A WOMAN'S WARNING

Eight women dressed in mannish-style riding outfits trotted along the main street of Cottonwood Springs. The auburn-haired leader signaled a halt. One of several hardcases took a step off the boardwalk and touched a hand to his hat brim.

"Y'all come to help us rob a bank?" he asked sneeringly.

"No," Charity Rose answered. "We came to serve you notice that your time has run out. Gather your gear and be out of town within an hour."

A sudden realization struck the outlaw as he studied Charity's face. "Say, you're the one Baudine said to look out for. Chestnut hair, green eyes, a damn big dog. Sister, you done come to the wrong place."

His Merwin and Hulbert .44 Pocket Army cleared leather ahead of Charity's Lightning. Before he raised it to her level, the lighter .38 barked twice. Dark spots appeared on his chest, yet the six-gun continued its upward arc. Charity shot again, hot lead entering his left eye socket.

"You men are on warning. You have an hour to leave town or die like your friend. I'm gonna clean out this rat's nest once and for all . . ."

WHITE SQUAW
Zebra's Adult Western Series
by E. J. Hunter

#1: SIOUX WILDFIRE	(1205, $2.50)
#2: BOOMTOWN BUST	(1286, $2.50)
#3: VIRGIN TERRITORY	(1314, $2.50)
#4: HOT TEXAS TAIL	(1359, $2.50)
#5: BUCKSKIN BOMBSHELL	(1410, $2.50)
#6: DAKOTA SQUEEZE	(1479, $2.50)
#10: SOLID AS A ROCK	(1831, $2.50)
#11: HOT-HANDED HEATHEN	(1882, $2.50)
#12: BALL AND CHAIN	(1930, $2.50)
#13: TRACK TRAMP	(1995, $2.50)
#14: RED TOP TRAMP	(2075, $2.50)
#15: HERE COMES THE BRIDE	(2174, $2.50)

Available wherever paperbacks are sold, or order direct from the Publisher. Send cover price plus 50¢ per copy for mailing and handling to Zebra Books, Dept. 2261, 475 Park Avenue South, New York, N.Y. 10016. Residents of New York, New Jersey and Pennsylvania must include sales tax. DO NOT SEND CASH.

#3 HARD-RIDING POSSE

E. J. HUNTER

ZEBRA BOOKS
KENSINGTON PUBLISHING CORP.

Special acknowledgment to Mark K. Roberts for his contribution to this work.

ZEBRA BOOKS

are published by

Kensington Publishing Corp.
475 Park Avenue South
New York, NY 10016

Copyright © 1988 by E. J. Hunter

All rights reserved. No part of this book may be reproduced in any form or by any means without the prior written consent of the Publisher, excepting brief quotes used in reviews.

First printing: January 1988

Printed in the United States of America

This volume in the adventures of Charity Rose is dedicated to Dixie Bowers, a good friend and the best receptionist any doctor could ever have.

EJH

Chapter One

Firm and steady, the wind set the pine boughs to gossiping. They spoke of things eternal, in whispers, sighs and moans. The aroma of pine pitch hung heavily around the small cabin in the hills of eastern Texas. Two horses, one of them a powerfully built black gelding, stood hipshot in a small corral. Their owners, inside the cabin, found other, more entertaining things to do than swat flies and munch oats.

"Oh! Yes, Bobby, deeper," the attractive, auburn-haired young woman pleaded as she drove her pelvis upward to meet him.

Leather straps, which supported the thin mattress pad, creaked and groaned beneath them. Beads of perspiration stood out on their healthy, naked bodies. Rigid muscles rippled on the supple frame of the hawk-nosed young man.

"Charity, Charity, you feel so good," Bob Carroll crooned as he plunged to the depths.

Stars exploded in their heads a few moments later, their long, languid period of love at last brought to a joyous conclusion. Idly Bob reached up and toyed with a lock of her deep amber hair.

"Seems to me both of us have recovered quite well," he observed.

Charity Rose fixed her sea green eyes on Bob's handsome face. His square jaw, crackling black eyes, full, sensuous lips and ready smile agreed mightily with her. They had been lovers for better than two months, since before the end of the Carroll-Wilkes feud and the breakup of the Concho Bill Baudine gang, since before Bob and Charity had both been wounded in the effort to rid the Longview, Texas area of outlaws and the jackals who traveled with them to enrich themselves on the spoils.

Their campaign succeeded, and now they reaped the rewards. Charity stretched, catlike, then elevated one curvaceous, creamy-complexioned thigh and draped it over Bob's hip. Slowly she began to impale herself on his bounty.

"Again?" Bob gasped.

"Oh, yes, Bobby. Again, and again, forevermore," Charity sighed.

Hank Rasmussen had taken a job with the new stage line because it offered excitement like the regular runs never did any more. Skirting the edge of Indian Territory, the Atwater Coach Company route promised the fastest way to Denver, Santa Fe and points west. It also left crew and passengers easy prey to border ruffians, highwaymen and occasional parties of Kiowa bucks. Few, if any of these, would risk his 10-gauge L. C. Smith, Hank had found out. It would take a large, organized and disciplined group to do that.

On a bright, sweet-smelling morning in late June, Hank Rasmussen and the passengers on the Columbine Number Four run to Denver came upon just such a group. Five large men, in trail-stained gray linen dusters, faces masked by bandanas, gray beaver felt Stetsons pulled low over mean, hollow eyes, sat horses across the road. Ten more appeared along both sides, forming an open-ended box into which the coach careered while Sam Pickles, the driver, tried to slow the team. Hanks shouldered his shotgun only to be flung backward, a sharp pain in his left shoulder, a moment before he heard the crack of the Winchester.

"Stand and deliver!" a daunting figure in the center of the road demanded in a deep voice.

"Whoa . . . waoh-up, Nel, Skeeter, Ike. Whoa!" Sam Pickles called to his six-up team. "Say, mister, you done picked the wrong coach. We ain't got a strongbox aboard," Sam addressed the apparent leader.

"The Lord punishes those who lie," a young outlaw named K. C. Honeywell said a split second before he shot Sam between the eyes.

"Hey, now, no call for that," a frightened, hurting Hank Rasmussen appealed.

"Keep quiet or you'll get it, too," the leader ordered. "Now, throw down the money box. And get the one from inside, too."

Warily, hampered by the wound in his shoulder, Hank laid aside his L. C. Smith and hauled out the company strongbox. He dumped it over the side to strike heavily on the ground. Hank turned to the road agents.

"I can't get down too easily with this hole in me. The Treasury box is under the front seat."

"All right, folks, everyone out of the coach," the leader demanded. "K. C., Buell, you get that other chest."

Two of the outlaws dismounted as the passengers clamored from the interior. The road agents stepped inside and wrenched the padded seat off its frame, then dumped it on the ground. From the recess within, they drew a heavy chest.

"It's here, Bill, like he said," K. C. Honeywell shouted.

"Good. Get it and the other one over to the horses. Now, folks," the leader turned his attention to the passengers, "it's your turn to donate."

"See here," a portly, florid-faced gentleman with a large sample case of various liquors expostulated. "Robbing the stage company, or the U.S. Treasury for that matter, is one thing. Taking our personal belongings is unconscionable."

"Those is mighty fancy words for a man 'bout to die," K. C. Honeywell observed. "I wunner if God'll unnerstan' 'em?"

Before the indignant whiskey drummer could form a response, K. C. Honeywell shot him twice in the chest.

"Go easy, K. C.," a masked bandit complained. "There ain't enough for ever'body as it is."

Two women, who had cried out in fright at the cold-blooded murder of the traveling salesman, huddled in each other's arms, sobbing. K. C. approached them and prodded one with his hot-barreled six-gun.

"C'mon, ladies. Empty your purses."

In no time, the gang had collected all the valuables and emptied the strongboxes. Then the killing began.

"Look at this," Charity Rose remarked to Bob Carroll over breakfast on the last day of June. "It seems your feud with the Wilkeses isn't the only one."

"What's that, honey?" Bob asked languidly, drowsy after a night of love-making.

"I'll read it to you. It's reprinted from the *New York Tribune*. 'Kansas is again in the saddle. Once more a four-mule team is attached to one of the courthouses and is going across the prairie at a fast trot. The existence of the western Kansas courthouse is at best transitory and uncertain. The golden morning sunlight floods it in Pottawatomie City, but its lengthning evening shadow falls across the streets of Little Paradise Valley. One day the stray swine of Occidental City seek its hospitable shade; the next, some predatory calf in Big Stranger bunts open the back door and eats the deed and two mortgages while the registrar is taking a nap. Today we mark it in Grand Junction with a new front door painted yellow, but tonight a band of determined men will come from Rattlesnake Crossing and haul it away with a yoke of oxen, with the mayor and city council of Rattlesnake pushing on the end of the courthouse. The Kansas courthouse is the Wandering Jew among public institutions.'

"It goes on to say that there are at least four counties in which two or more communities are fighting over where the county seat will be. Some have employed more police. Others are hiring gunfighters to 'protect' their claim."

"That's a lot of fuss over nothing, I'd say," Bob remarked.

"It has to have some importance," Charity persisted. "Otherwise people wouldn't get so upset over it."

Bob made a depreciating shrug. "You know people," he concluded.

Charity read on. "Here's something about the people I do know. 'The sole survivor of a stagecoach robbery identified the outlaws involved as the Concho Bill Baudine gang from names the road agents used during the commission of their savage crime. Two strongboxes and the personal valuables of the passengers were taken before the gang brutally gunned down the driver, guard and other passengers.' I knew Concho Bill would surface sometime soon. This places him in the Panhandle. I'm going after him, Bobby." Charity pushed back her chair.

"Now? Right this minute?" Bob Carroll inquired, clasping her about the waist and drawing her near.

Charity kissed him lightly on the lips several times. "No, not quite that fast. My guess is he'll head for Kansas. Hiring out to one of those towns disputing the county seat would be right in style for Bill. I can take the train tomorrow for Dallas."

Bob frowned, unhappy at her eagerness. Then he

brightened. "At least there'll still be time for . . . time for us?" he prompted.

Charity's face blossomed. "Of course there will. All of today and tonight. Oh, we haven't time to waste. I must pack and make arrangements."

"Slow down, honey. First on the list is a little loving."

"Outside. Let's go out under the trees," Charity urged, catching at Bob's hands.

Bob brought along a blanket, which he spread under their favorite old pine. Its wide, low-slung boughs soughed hauntingly in the breeze and perfumed the air with an exhilarating scent. Slowly, almost dreamily, Charity began to undress. Bob watched avidly, thrilled at each revelation. Pert, upthrust breasts, not excessively large, but firm and full, excited an instant response. Heat radiated from his loins, and his manhood began to lengthen and grow firm. Charity removed her skirt and stood spread-legged before him. Hands behind her, on the firm mounds of her buttocks, she leaned backward, her nipples pointed like gun muzzles at the sky.

Her auburn hair fluttered in the light zephyrs, and she wriggled with the joy of freedom as she removed the last of her clothing. Charity shivered with delight and spread her legs wider. Bob began to shake with unbearable desire as she cupped her breasts, then slid her hands down her lean, muscular torso.

Slowly Charity began to explore and stroke her silken flesh. Fully aroused, Bob's phallus strained painfully against his trousers. Quickly he removed his shirt and slid from his boots, trousers, and underdrawers. His own nakedness thrilled Charity, who gazed avidly at his hard, muscular body.

"I used to enjoy this so much when I was little," Charity stated in a drifting, dreamy voice. "Oh, when I was eleven, twelve, or so. It seemed to be the most wonderful fun in the world and here *I* had invented it, discovered it for the first time ever. I had no idea that every kid had some way of doing it. Until . . . until . . ."

"Yeah, until Corey came along," Bob said, a surly note in his voice.

"Bobby, you can't be jealous of a little boy, and what happened six years ago," Charity chided.

"I know I shouldn't be," Bob relented. "But I am . . . a little."

Charity stepped close to him, opened her arms and coaxed him in close. The heat of his passion registered on her creamy skin. Suddenly she wanted him so badly, all of him, deep within her.

"Think of it this way," she murmured in his ear. "If it hadn't been for Corey, I might never have fully awakened. He—he was even more scared and embarrassed than I. Truth to tell, I—I had it all planned out, couldn't wait for a chance to try it out on him."

"Thirteen-year-old girls shouldn't be contriving such things," Bob said primly, though he felt an overpowering urge to violently ravage her. "And boys that age shouldn't be indulging in them."

"I know," Charity responded contritely. "But after that first time, clumsy and scary as it was, Corey and I couldn't stop. We couldn't get enough, ever. Once I knew it was great fun, all the old wives' tales about the terrible burden of womankind could never destroy my pleasure. I simply didn't believe them because I *knew better*. At least until . . . until . . ."

Dark memories flooded Charity's mind, of that horrible day in the summer of her sixteenth year when the Baudine gang came to Dos Cabezas, Arizona Territory to break Concho Bill and two of his followers out of jail. They'd murdered her father before her eyes and then defiled her until she bled and ached for days after. It had been a long time before her healthy, passionate nature exerted itself. She'd feared she could never stand a man's touch again.

How wonderful her new freedom was when she once more allowed her urges to lead her into the sharing of carnal pleasure. There had been other men since, but Bob Carroll was the best, the most wonderful and caring of all. He gently stroked her hair now, aware of the demons that haunted her, and muttered soothing words.

The most wonderful of them came when she heard him softly urge, "Come, come, let me take the hurt away. I want to make you happy."

Kissing, they sank to their knees. Wildly stimulated by his touch, the firm presence of his manhood, Charity arranged herself to receive him fully as they were. Yes, she thought as the world whirled away, there'd be time for packing later.

Chapter Two

Rolling away from the Texas hills behind a sparkling new Baldwin 4-6-2 locomotive that was powerful enough to pull twenty cars, Charity Rose let the tantalizing memories of her delightful sojourn with Bob Carroll drift through a contented mind. Up ahead in the stock car, Butch and Lucifer rode in relative comfort. She did likewise, in a plush parlor car, compliments of the Longview banking members of the Carroll family. Her efforts in ending the Carroll-Wilkes feud and revitalizing the land development of the East Texas Cherokees had earned her a great deal of gratitude. Hence her own private coach at the end of the train.

It had advantages like real plush velvet chairs, arranged around small, glowing rosewood tables. She sat in one now, sipping a cool glass of lemonade and watching the scenery slide by. Memories of the past mingled, as they usually did, with erotic thoughts of the present . . .

. . . Sunlight bounced a thousand diamond shards off the water in the Los Padres Tanks, eroded basins in the bedrock filled by snowmelt and the infrequent rains of Arizona. Corey Willis lay on his back, naked on a bed of grass under the huge old cottonwood. He wriggled uncomfortably as Charity Rose, equally bare, tried to straddle his hips.

"It ain't gonna work," Corey pouted, the pink crescent

of his lower lip protruding. "Don't seem natural."

"Oh, c'mon, Corey. I want to try it," Charity begged as she lowered herself.

Tingles of joy shocked them both, as they always did, when their bodies first touched.

It was the occasion of Corey's fourteenth birthday. They had been avid lovers for a year, since their first shy experimentation. Now Charity wanted to give him a special gift. Slowly she impaled herself, then begun to rock. With a start, she suddenly realized that Corey had *grown* down there as well as in stature since the last summer. In spite of his mood, Corey soon joined in. Charity leaned back and looked down.

"Watch," she urged. "Watch how it works. We've never got to see it happen before."

Shyly, Corey glanced along the length of his slender, sun-browned body to where they joined in liquid friction. The sight shocked and thrilled him, and drove him quite wild.

"Oh, it's—it's . . . ah, Char, I never k-knew h-h-how great it is!" Corey cried, ending in a screech as he convulsed mightily and found release far too soon, overstimulated by the revelation . . .

. . . Bobby Carroll had really liked it that way too, Charity reflected happily. They'd spent many hours exploring and learning, sharing and giving. First and last. Somehow the enormous joy she had derived from both seemed symbolic. Perhaps at last her mind had healed; she no longer saw the body of, touch of, nor intimacy with a man as a threat. Oh, how she hoped so. The other way lay only loneliness.

Stop that, she chided herself. She rose and walked through the car, shaking off the mood. What would she choose for her meals? She wouldn't be into Dalllas until the next morning. Train travel, although pleasant, wasn't suited for her, Charity decided. It left her with nothing to do. Well, she reminded herself, she didn't have to stay in this car all alone. She could go exploring.

Through the efforts of the Temperance League and a number of fiery, persuasive preachers, Liberal, Kansas glowed with puritanical pride. The doors of the saloons had been shut and demon rum banished from the stomachs, if not the fond memories, of the male population. When this unusual and unexpected condition came to the attention of the Baudine gang, angry mutters went the rounds.

"Hell, a man can't even get a drink in this burg," Buell Nolan summed up for the others. "No use stayin' here."

"*Oui, mes amis,*" Frenchy Descoines rejoined. "But there is a nice little bank we can rob. Three banks, in fact."

"How are we goin' to hit three banks and get away safe?" Hal Newhouse demanded.

"Simple," Frenchy explained. "We rob them all at the same time. There are enough of us, *mais non?*"

"That's an ambitious undertaking, Frenchy," Concho Bill drawled, sure his friend had it all carefully planned out.

"We can do it, Bill. Trust me. Three men to each bank, three more to hold horses, and that leaves you and me to supervise and cover the escape route."

"Ummmm. Tell me more," Bill urged dryly.

"The best time to hit is shortly before closing time. Two close at three-thirty, one at four o'clock. So we rob them at exactly three-fifteen. In and out. Quite simple."

"Nobody's ever robbed three banks at the same time before," Newhouse protested.

"Does that mean it can't be done?" Frenchy countered. "If one were to believe the stories about Jesse James, *he* managed to rob three banks on the same day in three different towns, hundreds of miles apart. But that is the — how do you put it? — fiction written by newspapers. What I propose can be simply executed. Tomorrow is the day. And a fortuitous one at that. The city marshal is down with the gout and the county sheriff is off chasing some renegade Kiowas who crossed over from the Territory. We'll have little opposition, and none that is professional."

"How do you learn all these things in so short a time, Frenchy?" Newhouse asked sullenly.

"I use my eyes and my ears, *mais non?* I, ah, listen more than I talk," the New Orleans orphan turned outlaw responded, a sneer emphasizing the implied criticism. Then he turned to Nolan. "And for you, *mon ami*, there is an old man who lives on the east edge of town who doesn't agree with or approve of the temperance climate of Liberal. For a modest sum, he'll sell you all the whiskey you want, by the bottle."

All of a sudden, Buell Nolan looked chipper. "What're we waitin' for then?"

Midafternoon Kansas sun burned Liberal a sere brown on this first day of July. With the saloons closed and almost nowhere to turn for entertainment save the pool tables in the back of the barbershop, little traffic clogged the streets. Sapped by the enervating heat, few people paid attention to the groups of men who rode silently to each of the three banks in Liberal's downtown section. One rider in each quartet remained outside while the remaining trio dismounted and entered the cool interior of the brick-and-native-fieldstone structures. Little business seemed to be getting done in the oppressive hot spell. Things livened up some when one of the strangers remained by the front door while the other two walked to the tellers' cages.

When they got in position, the one at the entrance announced in a loud voice, "This is a holdup, folks. Everyone stay right where you are."

One clerk at the Farmers' Trust Bank, new on the job and insecure, made a grab for the six-gun in his cash drawer and received a revolver barrel behind one ear for his efforts. He fell to the floor like a bag of wet wash. The outlaw who had struck him pointed to the teller on his right with the muzzle of his .45 Colt.

"You. Empty out your drawer, then do his."

"When you boys finish, I'll cover 'em, while you clean out the vault," the one at the door announced.

"You'll never get away with this," the banker quavered, his voice made uncertain by age and fear.

The holdup men ignored him. Each went about his task with practiced precision. When they finished, they backed to the door and joined their companion.

"Now, I don't want any of you deciding to play hero. Nobody comes out that door in less than five minutes."

Then they scrambled for their horses.

At the other banks the robberies went much the same. A stray dog lifted its leg and urinated on the boot of the horse holder outside the Prairie Bank of Liberal. One swift kick sent it yipping down the street. A woman fainted in the Merchants' Consolidated Bank. Two stout matrons in bonnets and elbow-length capes, sweating profusely and pretending not to, started to enter the Merchants' Bank, saw what was in progress and tried to extricate themselves, only to run into the muzzle of Concho Bill Baudine's six-gun.

"Go on in, ladies," he commanded with a tip of his hat. "Join the fun."

By 3:27, the outlaw band had joined forces a block east of the Farmers' Trust Bank and were riding swiftly out of town. To their credit and advantage, considering the nature of many of the gang, not a shot had been fired—

though the angry, wounded screams of the bankers gave the impression that wholesale slaughter had been done.

Charity Rose selected a trail leading northwestward out of Dallas, which would take her into the Panhandle and the shortest way to the troubled counties of Kansas. She would, on the way, ask questions about the stage robbery. On her second day out, she came upon a family heading to the Palo Duro country, with all of their possessions piled high in a cut-down version of the Conestoga. The bearded, lanky man gave her a friendly hail, and his wife made her immediately welcome.

"It's so nice to see someone heading our way," Lucinda Collings told Charity gratefully. "Land, I reckoned we might be headed off the edge of the earth for all the people we've seen."

"We're in empty country, for sure, Lucinda." Charity agreed.

"Be stopping for our noonin' soon," Lucinda observed. "You're welcome to share beans and fatback with us, Charity."

"That's kind of you. I'd be happy to. I'll even put up some dried apples in a pot to make sauce to go with it."

"My that would be nice," Lucinda responded.

"Umm-yumm," ten-year-old Jimmy Collings added with approval. The carrot-top's freckled cheeks had been burned mightily by the sun, his button nose peeling.

His two sisters, younger than he, giggled their delight. When the caravan was halted and a fire set, Asa and Lucinda Collings came to where Rebecca rubbed down Lucifer's black hide. They held hands like shy youngsters and found trouble with their words.

"We were wondering, that is, if it isn't any imposition, and the children adore you, Charity . . . so—ah, we, ah, if it wouldn't be too far out of your way, would you be agreeable to accompany us to Mister Charley Goodnight's place in the Palo Duro?" Lucinda managed to stammer out.

"Well . . ." Charity speculated aloud. "It's not but a bit out of my way," she allowed. "And I'd be grateful for the company. It would be easier on Butch too, if he could ride the sling under your wagon."

"Oh, no trouble, no trouble at all," Asa Collings hastened to assure her.

"All right, then, I think we might just manage it."

Happiness and relief flooded the Collings' faces.

For the next two days, the journey remained uneventful. They'd soon come to the Red River country, and shortly after, the Palo Duro. Everyone relaxed. Then, in midmorning of the third day, with a small thunderstorm building to the southwest, a more tangible threat presented itself. Charity, riding slightly ahead, with Jimmy Collings astride a swaybacked plug, sighted some dozen indistinct figures in the wavering heat waves. Charity couldn't be sure, but she thought she saw feathers being used for adornment. She reached out a hand to Jimmy's bare, sunburned arm.

"Jimmy, turn around and ride back to the wagon. Tell your folks we've got some riders coming this way. I'll wait awhile and try to identify them, then join you."

"Injuns?" Jimmy asked, wide-eyed in excited anticipation.

"I certainly hope not," Charity confided. "If they are, we'll have to make the best of it. Now you scoot."

Hollering his news, Jimmy trotted off toward the wagon like any child his age. Charity watched him briefly, then returned her attention to the strange riders. For a while they grew steadily closer; then, hidden by a rise a quarter mile away, they disappeared. A worried frown creased Charity's brow. Intuitively, she turned Lucifer and hurried back to the wagon. The prairie birds had stopped their warbling and an ominous silence held by the time she reached there. She did not dismount, but rather turned Lucifer toward the sound of rumbling, unseen thunder.

With a *kiiiii-yaiii* and fearsome war whoops, half a dozen Kiowa warriors breasted a low, close-in ridge. The others remained out of sight, which caused Charity considerable concern. Those they could see charged toward the small caravan, brandishing their weapons. At once, Charity drew her Marlin Pacific rifle and chambered a round. Asa Collings did the same with his Winchester. Tensely they waited.

Clots of sod flying from their ponies' hoofs, the Kiowas came closer. They sent up fan-shaped sprays of dirt and grass when they halted stiff-legged only five yards from the worried whites. One of them, somewhat older than the others, gestured with his feather-decorated staff.

"Want caw-fee," he demanded in a quavery voice.

"Give food. Give beef," another, obviously the leader, commanded.

"We don't have any beef. Only the milk cow," Asa replied.

"Give beef, you live. No give beef, you die," the hard-faced leader stated flatly.

To emphasize his threat, he waved his feathered war lance over his head, and the other braves appeared along the top of the rise behind them. The leader looked over the whites he confronted. He paid particular attention to Jimmy Collings, who grimly held a small shotgun white-faced and shaking slightly. A smile creased the Kiowa's lips. He pointed to Jimmy.

"We trade. Take boy, give many fine buffalo robes. Two hands robes for boy. He make good son to me."

Charity had no experience with the Kiowa. Small in

stature for the most part, mean-faced and spare in frame, they reminded her of Apaches from Arizona. She wondered if they might react the same way to similar things.

"We don't trade off our children for robes," Charity stated sternly.

"You trade or die," came the final demand.

At this point, she concluded, anything would be worth a try. "Butch, *iamh*," she ordered her half-wolf canine companion. At once, Butch began to warily circle the Indians.

"Stop you dog," one of the party ordered uneasily.

"Not dog . . . wolf," Charity responded, taking a certain pleasure in the reaction of the Kiowas.

"Wolf no live by people," the leader stated flatly, more to reassure himself than from conviction.

"This one does," Charity retorted. "I trained him. He follows my orders."

Right then, Lucifer caught a full dose of Indian scent. His nostrils flared and he snorted, while his skin rippled like black water. Eyes rolling, mane bristled, he started forward.

"My horse has captured the spirit of a warrior, too. He will fight you." The leader started to signal for an attack, his features twisted into a mask of anger, when Charity fired nearly in his face. Pain registered in his hand and arm as lead struck the iron tip, snapping it off the lance, which he let go of as though it had burned him. At once, Butch became a gray-black streak that howled once, shortly, before savaging at the vulnerable hamstrings of the Kiowa horses.

Asa Collings coolly shot the bow from the hands of a warrior in the second, more distant group. By then the nearer band had their hands full with the pandemonium created by Butch's snapping teeth. Their mounts prancing and squealing, they hastily withdrew.

"Will they come back?" Lucinda Collings asked in a

frightened tone.

"I don't know," Charity told her. "We can only wait and see."

Chapter Three

Orin Meadows made his last rounds at midnight. The small pool hall-saloon, which served beer and a little whiskey, usually closed by ten o'clock. Orin always allowed ample time for any of the local jawers to finish their arguments and wend their way home before turning out the six kerosene lamps tht illuminated the main street of Hopewell, Kansas. Satisfied that his duty had been done, Orin would then go to his own lodging and let himself inside as quietly as possible.

He didn't want to awaken his wife and three children. At thirty-six, and still handsome, Orin Meadows had acquired streaks of gray at his temples and lines in his face. His wife of fourteen years had stood steadfast at his side through the hard years, borne his children — two girls and a boy — and made a home for him in one town after another. Not until arriving in Hopewell did she exhibit any stubbornness or show regret for the way of life of a roving peace officer. His way had become hers. Then, in Hopewell, with a nice school, three churches, two mercantiles, a butcher shop, millinery, haberdashery, lumberyard, and all the touches of civilization, she became adamant.

"This is where we stay Orin. I don't care what you might find in greener pastures, but this is it. Our children need schoolin'. Here they can get it. Tommy is eight, the girls six and five, and none of them have ever seen the inside of a schoolhouse for more than three months at a time. We don't move until the children have finished their schoolin'."

She'd made it stick. Orin became a deputy sheriff, then chief deputy; he had run for the office three years ago and been elected sheriff of Crowley County, Kansas. He had many friends and strong support. He saw it as a secure life. His wife loved it and praised the day they came to Hopewell. Then along came the county-seat wars.

The county had split almost fifty-fifty over the issue of what town would be the seat of government in Crowley County. It meant a great deal in money and allowances from the state. It could also attract a railroad through the lucky community. Several elections had been held to decide the issue, only to have the results declared null by the courts, which saw the proceedings as illegal. That left things up in the air. As had been his custom over the past few months of the disagreement, Orin brooded sourly on the circumstances while he completed his task and directed his long strides toward home. Ten minutes after entering his bedroom, Orin Meadows was snoring softly his cheek resting on his wife's soft brown hair.

He didn't hear the gentle, slow clop of hoofs as five men entered Hopewell from the southeast, from the direction of Cottonwood Springs. They reined their mounts to a pool of dark shadow at one side of the Crowley County Courthouse, located on the town square across from the Methodist church. Without a word, they dismounted and entered, each carrying a pair of saddlebags.

Inside, they went quickly to work, gathering all the county records and stuffing them into their saddlebags. The assessor's seal, the county commission's, the registrar of deeds' and other seals were also loaded into their leather pouches. Once this had been completed, a large can rattled and gurgled loudly, and the odor of kerosene permeated the air. With their saddlebags secured, the men made ready to depart.

"Go ahead, light it off," Karl Richter urged.

In answer a lucifer match flared, flickered feebly and settled into a small sphere of yellow light. The man who had fired it let it drop at the edge of a pool of kerosene. Yellow-orange wavered a moment, then grew up the spectrum into a nearly pure blue flame as the coal oil took hold.

"Let's get out of here," one night rider urged.

With considerably more noise than they had made when they entered, the Committee to Restore Cottonwood Springs galloped out of town. Behind them they left the flaming courthouse. In only moments the alarm sounded. Orin Meadows awakened groggily, yanked on a pair of trousers, fitted feet to boots and stumbled, yawning, onto the street.

In the distance, flames turned the city skyline red-orange. Meadows blinked owlishly and began to trot toward the center of the business district. The closer he came, the more he feared he knew the location and cause of the fire.

"Hey, Sheriff," a town loafer called. "It was some fellers I saw over Cottonwood Springs way. They rode in; fifteen minutes or so later, they rode out like the devil hisself was chasin' them."

"Thank you, Spooner. Anyone else get a look at who did it?" Meadows inquired in a loud voice.

Silence answered while flames licked at the courthouse. The city's volunteer fire department had the pumper there, men swinging rhythmically on the bars that controlled the pressure pump. A bucket brigade had formed, with double rows of men and boys swinging buckets from the town well. Bit by bit, the wall of flame diminished.

The roar became a crackle. Brightness dimmed. The whirlwinds of sparks ceased. By a miracle of determination and experience, the firefighters quenched the blaze. Word went out quickly, as to the suspected source. Angry voices carried the news, along with a growing intention.

"We'll fix 'em for that."

"Those Cottonwood Springs ya-hoos can't get away with this."

"The county seat's gonna be *here,* if we have to wring all their necks in Cottonwood Springs."

Line riders had greeted them first. Their welcome had been nothing like this. Word had quickly spread so that by the time Charity Rose and the Collings family reached the main ranch house of the Palo Duro, a laughing, shouting throng, mostly women and children, waited to accept them into the fold. Charley Goodnight himself, with his beard, thick thatch of dark hair and twinkling blue eyes, set the mood by embracing Lucinda and Charity, and slapping Asa on the back.

"I hear you saved my people here from the Kiowas," Goodnight addressed Charity.

"Well, not exactly, Mister Goodnight. I did convince them it would be to their advantage not to attack us. Or rather, my dog did."

"How's that?" Charley Goodnight inquired, eyeing Butch askance. "He looks more wolf than dog," he added dubiously.

"He is," Charity answered. "I set him on the hamstrings of the Kiowa ponies. They didn't like that very much and took off without robbing us."

"Or worse, young lady," Charley Goodnight snapped back. "Well then, we'll have to save a special, juicy bone with lots of meat on it for you, feller," he concluded.

"His name's Butch," Charity advised Goodnight.

"Ummm, fits," Charley responded. "Part wolf, eh? Damn, but you must have a way with animals."

"I raised him from a puppy. He was hurt and abandoned and I cared for him."

"Small wonder he's loyal to you, Miss Charity. Take a leg off anyone else, I'd reckon," Goodnight opined.

"Right you are, Mister Goodnight," she agreed.

"Now, before you go gettin' itchy-footed, let me tell you what's in store," the bubbly, big-shouldered rancher informed Charity. "First off, I'm gonna send some vaqueros out to find a prime steer. Then we're gonna butcher it, and maybe some goats to go along, and build a huge fire in the pit over there. We're gonna cook him up Texas-style and serve it off with all the trimmin's. We're gonna have a fiesta you'll not forget in a month of Sundays."

Caught up in the spirit and enthusiasm of the rancher, Charity responded with excitement of her own. "That sounds like my kind of fun, Mister Goodnight. You might even talk me into dancing a turn or two."

What followed, a fiesta of truly Texan proportions, astonished even Charity, who had recently been entertained in the same grand style at Longview. But Longview was not nearly so elaborate as this, she soon discovered. The celebration lasted through the rest of that day, the night and the next day. Chickens and corn roasted in large clay ovens. The spit turned constantly, burdened with a whole steer and two goats, over a large bed of coals. Pies and cakes began to appear on the large trestle tables, along with bowls of beans cooked half a dozen ways; rice, steamed or fried with tomatoes, chili peppers and onions; fresh, hot, flat tortillas; bowls of chili sauce and Mexican *salsa;* diced cactus; and pickled peppers. And with it all, the exact and proper thing to drink.

Tamarind water, manzanilla tea, beer, wine, tequila, they all paraded the bountiful table. The music turned out to be a haunting mixture of Highland ballads, primitive Indian rhythms, the gypsy music of Spain and that peculiar blend of all of them, the mariachi music of Mexico.

Enchanted by the carefree blend of cultures, Charity enjoyed everything immensely. A favorite with the Palo Duro cowboys, she danced until her legs ached, ate her fill from the heavily laden tables, and danced some more.

"Miss Charity, how d'you like entertainin' Panhandle-style?" the Palo Duro home-ranch foreman inquired as he whirled her around in a reel.

"This is . . ." Charity fought to form the right words. "This is as big as Texas."

"Thought y'all would like it. Gonna stay with us awhile?"

Charity paused a moment before answering that. She hadn't considered the possibility. "Well, not really. I, ah, have something I wanted to look into up Kansas way."

Chris Anderson, the foreman, frowned. "Oh, yeah. I heard something about that from Asa Collings. Don't seem right, a pretty young gal like yourself chasin' outlaws."

Charity arched an eyebrow. "I should leave it up to ugly old gals?" she asked teasingly.

Chris blushed. "You're funnin' me, Miss Charity."

"That I am. C'mon now, Chris. I want to forget all that for a while and enjoy this party."

High and steep, carved by millennia of erosion from the Red River, the particolored walls of Palo Duro Canyon echoed the revelry. When at last the celebration wound down and everyone benefitted from some much-needed rest, Charity thanked her host and the new friends she'd made, saddled up and made ready to depart northward toward Kansas.

Bat Masterson, Billy Tilghman and Jim Marshall had

all signed on in Dodge City. Asa T. Soule, entrepreneur of Ingalls, Kansas, journeyed to Dodge and other tough towns in order to obtain assistance in the Gary County disagreement over whether Ingalls or Cimarron would be the county seat. Following elections, court orders and finally a session before the State Supreme Court—which had ordered the election to stand, with Ingalls the rightful winner—the titles, deeds and police court records remained in Cimarron. The decision had been made to take them by force. The notorious gunmen were to be in Ingalls one week from the date of being contacted.

"Might be this could turn into a regular shootin' war," Bat Masterson observed to his two friends as they stood at the bar in the Oasis Saloon in Dodge City.

"Soule didn't hire us to *talk* those Cimarron folks out of the county records," observed Bill Tilghman, who had sold the Oasis to his brother Frank not long ago. "If it weren't for that court order, I'd have nothing to do with it."

The youngster of the trio, the fair-haired, tall, thin Bill Tilghman watched his friends closely. Dapper as always in a dark suit, trim vest and snowy white stiff-front shirt, William Barclay Masterson wore his derby hat at a rakish angle and propped his silver-headed cane against the front of the mahogany bar. His frock coat covered the butt of a well-worn and well-cared-for .45 Colt. Jim Marshall, a lawman for over thirty years, dressed similarly, but without as much style and expense. His string tie drooped over a soft-collar shirt, and signs of wear made his suit coat glossy in spots. He wore his six-gun well forward, the butt canted out beyond his body. Gray streaked his hair, and his sun-leathered face carried a plethora of squint and smile wrinkles. To a stranger, none of the three had the look of the most proficient gunfighter in the state.

"Letter-of-the-Law Tilghman, we'll have to call you," Jim Marshall taunted him. "Truth is, they ain't payin' us all that much. So I suppose there's a little of that abidin' by the law in all of us on this thing." He eyed his companions owlishly as he stroked his white goatee.

"There's some who'd say the law is corrupt in this matter," Masterson observed, brushing at his luxuriant black mustache. "That resisting the law in this particular case is the right and noble thing."

Jim Marshall shrugged, indifferent. "Then that's where the shootin' war comes in."

"Who all we be workin' with?" Billy Tilghman inquired.

"George Bolds, Ed Brooks, Neal Brown," Masterson listed them. "Fred Singer, and several others I've not been told of so far."

"Will the Gary County sheriff back our play?" Tilghman asked.

Bat flashed a broad smile. "Far as I know he will. He lives in Ingalls and voted for the town's proposal as county seat."

"That's one thing," Tilghman observed. "Shootin' up another town to take away the records could be another to his way of seein' it."

"Well, that's something," Bat declared, "that we'll just have to wait and see about."

"*Scheisse!* Vat ve're doing is against the law," Otto Blutcher protested. "Sure, now ve have the county records and Cottonwood Springs is the county seat. But vat if those *hunden* from Hopewell come after vat ve took?"

"Then we fight for it," Karl Richter said forcefully. He pounded one big ham fist on the polished oak of a table usually used by the defendant and counsel in the courthouse. It had also been removed from Hopewell. "Otto, we have invested too much, taken too many chances to fail now."

"The most of people don't know vat ve've put into this, Karl."

"And we'd better hope that they never find out, Otto. You're not having second thoughts, are you?"

"*Nein,*" Otto answered vehemently. "I'll see it through. Only ve don't vant any killing. Ve agreed, Karl."

Otto looked imploringly at his fellow conspirator. Karl Richter's usually florid complexion had become beet-hued, his small, piggy eyes glittering a malevolent blue in their deep sockets. Black hair fell in a thick shock over the left side of his forehead, and his moon face with its heavy jowls held a certain menace. The effect prompted Otto to repeat his declaration.

"Ve agreed, Karl, no killing, no one gets hurt, *ja?*"

"No one gets hurt," Karl agreed. "Yet, if they use force to try to recover the records and furniture, we will be compelled to do whatever is necessary to keep everything here."

Otto's light, sun-reddened complexion paled at this pronouncement. The fat, fiftyish man didn't like the sound of that at all. He laced big, beefy fingers over the swell of his paunch under the bib overalls and glowered at his partner. Surely, he sought to convince himself, Karl could be reasoned with. Even if matters grew worse. They had the records. That should be the end of it. Despite his effort to remain optimistic, a cold spot within him mocked that idea as simplistic.

Chapter Four

Outside of the small hand-lettered sign beside the trail, nothing indicated any sort of change. Thornbush, sage and cactus dotted the sandy yellow-brown soil, and heat waves shimmered, obscuring everything in the distance. Charity Rose read the sign again before pressing on.

INDIAN TERRITORY
Settlement by Whites
Prohibited by Federal Law.
Permission to cross land
subject to approval of the
Army and Tribal Councils.
Address inquiries: Commandant,
Fort Sill, Indian Territory.

Not the most welcoming of notices, she considered. Her packhorse had bent its long neck to the ground and nibbled at grass around one of the rough, circular posts that supported the sign. Butch eyed the other a moment, lifted his leg and irrigated the warning with unerring accuracy.

"C'mon, Butch, Lucifer. We want to be well away from here before sundown," she said aloud.

Hours of riding made little change in the scenery. Charity hummed snatches of several popular songs, talked to Butch and Lucifer and watched the flat, red-brown earth go by. Vultures hovered high in the air, seeking some sort of properly decomposed prey. A redtailed hawk circled lower, spotted movement and dived swiftly, to rise a second later, a twitching mouse in its talons. Some three hours before sundown, Charity noticed a profuse column of smoke some distance ahead.

Not too smart, Charity allowed, considering the location. About all such a poorly maintained fire could attract here would be trouble. From Indian or white, it mattered little. She uttered a derisive grunt at her foolishness and pointed Lucifer toward the inept travelers. The least she could do, she argued to herself, would be to get them to curtail that smoke.

From a hundred yards out, Charity recognized the figures of several women. That puzzled her, considering only two wagons could be seen near the fire. At fifty yards, she reined in and hailed the strangers.

"Hello, the camp!"

A profusion of squeals and excited chatter answered her. Charity could now make out some seven females clustered about, gawking in her direction and waving. Another joined them, then a man. His voice rang out over the prairie.

"Howdy, stranger. Ride on in and get yerself a treat."

That didn't make much sense. Charity shrugged and trotted Lucifer in closer. Dressed in her trail clothes, her hair tucked up under her tan Stetson, she cut a definitely mannish figure. At her approach, the feminine figures resolved into individual features. They all seemed eager to see her. Several waved; all primped and made bold, provocative gestures. Drawing nearer, Charity noted that all appeared to be quite young and shapely, with uniformly pretty faces.

No, not exactly pretty. Several had "painted on" good looks. Behind the cosmetics, they must have revealed more age than their physiques implied. Whatever had she come upon? Charity pondered as she traversed the last few yards into camp. Grinning wolfishly, the man came out of the swirl of women and swiped his hat off his head.

"Welcome, stranger. Lane Everets' the name. Step down and avail yourself of the vast plenty of pulchritude. It's your lucky day. Look around and take your choice. You can have your wildest dreams fulfilled for the modest sum, considering how far we're removed from civilization, of only five dollars gold."

With the numbing speed and impact of a lightning bolt, Charity Rose understood what she had encountered. She'd ridden into a caravan of traveling tarts. These women, with their provocative poses, enticing expressions and lascivious looks, were one and all soiled doves, the inmates of a mobile bordello. Humor quickly replaced her shocked surprise, and Charity pulled off her hat to let auburn locks spill lushly down from the crown of her head.

"Whatever would I want with that?" she inquired.

Lane Everets' jaw sagged. He blinked and produced a rodentlike leer, small black eyes glittering with lust. The prospective customer had turned out to be a real looker. Now that the auburn tresses gave definition to the soft lines of the face, he could readily see he had before him a true wonder. Her smile, taunting, teasing, though not unkind, could thaw the heart of a misanthrope. Sea green eyes, intriguing and seemingly bottomless. . . . Everets ached with the desire to have the clothes off of her, get a good look at the rest of her body.

Heat radiated from his loins and his member began to stiffen at these thoughts. Yes, he'd have to get closer to this remarkable number. She would become prime merchandise. She'd be good for four, five, maybe six years. Put hundreds of dollars in Lane Everets' pocket. Cautioning himself to move slowly, not frighten the quarry away, Everets spoke ungently.

"Ummm, ah, well, yes, let me introduce my girls." Nine of them stood in a tight half-circle around Charity and Lane. Everets began on the left and gave out names as he went along.

"This is Fleur, Babette, Antoinette, Gigi, Clarisse, Evette, Nichole, Adrianne, and Monique," Everets introduced over their constant, shrill chatter.

"Oh, they're all French," Charity blurted. It elicited a round of giggles and another babble of shrill voices.

"Not a French lady among them," Everets came back. "It's fashionable among those who visit sporting houses to be entertained by ladies with French names. Gives their liaison a touch of class."

"I, ah, I see. I'm Charity Rose, ladies," Charity stumbled through her embarrassment.

Another chorus of shrieking delight. "It's a natural, dearie," an older soiled dove declared huskily. "I can see it now," she went on, arms describing a large, lighted marquee. "Charity Rose. Tantalizing delight of the Ooold Souuuuth. Why hush my mouth, honey chile."

"Zelda's right," another bawd enthused. "You'd have men standin' in line all night."

"Ah, girls, girls," Lane Everets interrupted, "how about giving Charity room to breathe. Step back. What's your pleasure, Charity? We've got coffee boilin', some good stone-crock cider and a pitcher of lemonade."

"I think you all have the wrong idea," Charity answered hastily. "I didn't come to *join* you, ah, ladies. I'm only passing through."

"That's what *I* said, seven years ago," Zelda came back. "Once you get started, it sort of, ah, grows on you, believe me."

Charity tried again. "What I came here for was to tell you that your fire is too smoky. We're in Indian Territory here and you can never tell what might happen. Too much smoke draws curious people."

"Well, goldarn it, what can we do? We don't know about things like that," Zelda said defensively.

"I do," Charity told them simply. "That's what I came over for, to give you a hand. That is, if you'll let me."

"Let you? You can take over the whole awful mess. We ain't accustomed to makin' our livin' bendin' over a steaming pot of stew."

"Yeah," Babette added on. "We've got more comfortable positions to work in."

Another chorus of giggles filled the small stand of cottonwood trees where camp had been laid out. Charity ignored the bawdy banter, wondering how these young women could make light of their situation. Unaccustomed to ending the day so early, Butch went off, sniffing along invisible trails, in search of a rabbit or two. Charity began instructing them in proper fire building while correcting theirs. She suggested that for really good stew, or whatever they intended for the evening meal, a few wild onions, turnips and the like thrown in would improve the flavor. While she conducted her class in frontier living, Lane Everets looked on from a distance and formulated a plan of his own.

"She's quite a looker, wouldn't you say?" he asked of Penelope Saunders, who billed herself as Gigi.

Somewhat older than most of the girls, Penelope had developed hardness around her eyes—and her soul, for that matter. She was losing her youthful appeal, her mouth curving down in cynical distaste, eyes empty and mocking. Over the years, Lane had come to confide in her as he would in a partner. She alone among the girls realized how hopeless their futures were, how empty their dreams. Everets shared his thoughts with her now as the idea came alive in his brain.

"Bit on the tough side, wouldn't you say?" she asked back.

Everets smiled. "That's a mere exterior, my dear. I'd

venture to say that underneath, she's hot as fireworks on the Fourth. Get those men's clothes off her . . ."

"You'd like that, wouldn't you?" Penelope quipped.

"I won't deny that. I'd like to get control of her. Turn her out at our next stop on the tour."

"You're a cold bastard, Lane. You wouldn't be seeking to replace me, now I'm getting older, eh?"

"Nothing of the kind," Everets hastened to declare. "I'm only thinking of increasing our income."

"How would you go about it?" Penelope asked.

"That . . . I don't know as yet. I'll think of something. It would help if you went over there and got friendly with her," Everets suggested.

"I can do that, all right," Penelope agreed.

After supper, talk turned to the girls and their past lives. Their revelations surprised, and sometimes shocked, Charity. Except for Penelope Saunders—Gigi—none of the soiled doves was over twenty-one. All had been in the business for at least five years. Babette's story intrigued and horrified Charity most of all.

"My real name is Charlene. Charlene Cramer," Babette began shyly. "My friends call me Charlie. I've been in this business for eight years."

Charity could hardly believe it. Actually, she had to admit, Charlie looked hardly over thirteen as it was. A real looker, with big blue eyes, an angelic smile and long, pale blond hair, she barely stood five-foot-four, with a narrow waist and small breasts, which gave her a little-girl look.

"H-how did you get started so young?" Charity asked her.

Charlie lowered long lashes, then glanced up at Charity with an urchin appeal. Lips slightly parted to reveal tiny nubbins of even white teeth, she let her mind slip backward, recalling the past.

"We lived in St. Louis. Poppa had left us by then," she

said in a far-off voice. "It had been a hard winter and Momma was down with the wastin' sickness. There was eight of us kids. Emil, who was a year older than me, was already workin' at what he could. Still we needed more money comin' into the house. Bein' second oldest, it was up to me to provide it.

"Now, there isn't much a girl of thirteen can do for a living. I'd already entertained a few boys, and even two growed men. The men offered me money for my favors, so I knew all about that. Didn't take me long to be bringin' twenty, twenty-five dollars a week in to help pay for food and medicine. That was more cash money than we'd ever seen, even when Poppa was to home. Soon I learned all kinds of tricks to please a man." "That's so sad," Charity remarked softly. "Such an awful sacrifice for any little girl to make. Surely you've become disillusioned by now?" she prompted.

"Oh, no. Somewhere along the line I began to like it. Now I can't get enough. What I want, what I dream of, is opening a place of my own someday."

"Charlie!" Charity exclaimed, her modest upbringing rebelling at this revelation. "That's awful. Yet . . . yet," she grudgingly admitted, "I can't help being a little bit envious."

"What about me?" Helen Moran—Antoinette to her clientele—inquired, a bit offended. "*I* didn't strut around like a strumpet." Her challenge had no effect on bright-eyed Charlie. "I got forced into the business. By my own family, at that."

"They set you up in business?" Charity asked, not believing.

"No. My parents sold me into a brothel."

The statement, delivered without emotional coloring, stunned Charity. "But, that's . . . that's *slavery*. Nobody could do a thing like that."

"Call it what you want, that's what they did. There

were too many of us and no money. I grew up in Juarez, across from El Paso, Texas. My father took me to this woman one day, just after I turned eleven. He got money and I became an inmate of the *putaría*. Our family name was Morano. I dropped the 'oh' when I came across the border."

Helen's long black hair, shiny obsidian eyes, and high cheekbones bore witness to the veracity of her claim. Charity's heart ached for Helen's tragic past. She wanted to protect the unfortunate young woman, help her find a better way of life. Yet Helen's last statement created another question.

"Helen, after you crossed the border," Charity probed, "why didn't you find some other way to earn a living?"

Helen shrugged. "What else did I know to do? There I was, fourteen years old. I'd run away from a Mexican whorehouse, I was in this country without papers. So I took a job in a saloon."

"I—I feel so sorry for you," Charity empathized.

"Don't. I'm no worse off than a lot of people. At least I eat regularly, have nice clothes and a roof over my head." Helen threw a glance at the wagons. "Even if it's on wheels a lot of the time."

While the women exchanged stories of their lives, Lane Everets set to achieving his goal. Unseen by the flock of lovelies around the fire, he blended a large dollop of laudanum with coffee and sugar in a cup. Grinning broadly, he brought it to Charity.

"I put a little drop of rum in it," he told her. "Helps you sleep soundly even when the coyotes raise a fuss."

"Why, thank you, Mr. Everets," Charity responded, taking the tin container.

She winced a moment later, when her lips closed on the metal rim. "Why is it that a person never thinks of the result when one puts hot liquid in a tin cup?"

Her question elicited a fit of giggles from the bevy of

bawds. Charity let the coffee cool slightly, then drank deeply of it. She looked around for Butch, then recalled that he had set off on a rabbit chase. Odd, she felt quite sleepy, she reflected. Good thing Lucifer had been cared for. She drank again and felt herself sway slightly on the rounded top of a portmanteau set out for a chair. Any more of this and she'd rudely fall asleep right in front of her hosts.

"Well, if any of you care at all," another soiled dove began, "what I thought was an elopement turned out to be getting stolen away to a . . ."

The words clicked off as Charity slid down into a pool of blackness. Lane Everets rushed forward, a coil of light rope in his hand.

"Hurry. A couple of you help me. We'll tie her up and get her in a wagon. I've now got me ten lovely ladies."

"Damn you, Lane," Zelda snapped. "You've never done anything like this before. Whatever possessed you . . ."

Everets' vicious backhand slap silenced Zelda's protest. A strawberry stain marred her smooth cheek. "Shut up and do as I say, gawdammit," he growled. "Be quick about it. We want to break camp at once and get on our way."

Under Lane's direction, Zelda and Helen tied Charity's hands and ankles. Everets then added a gag. "Don't want her sickin' that dog on me," he explained. "Now, help me lift her into the rear wagon."

Charity's slim waist and small stature proved a fooler. Her blocky strength, from hours of exercise and miles of riding, gave her more weight than could be reckoned. It took a lot of effort to get her head and shoulders over the tailgate of the wagon. Everets paused there to climb inside. A low growl brought him around, one leg hoisted to a wagon spoke.

Gold eyes burning hotly, long fangs exposed, Butch stood spraddle-legged near the fire. Gasps came from several of the youthful hookers, and they slowly backed away from the scene that attracted Butch's attention. Rabbit hunting forgotten, the half-wolf, half-mastiff braced to attack the one he perceived as threatening his mistress. Hair rose stiffly on his neck, and he braced to lunge.

In the fraction of a second before the fatal leap, Lane Everets drew his revolver and fired. Butch yelped pitifully and leaped upward, to fall back in a spray of blood from his neck. He kicked at the ground, seeking purchase to rise, then whined weakly and lay still. Lane Everets hastened to complete his task.

"Help me, dammit," he snapped. "That dog won't hurt anyone now. Get the teams hitched. Zelda, hoist her legs so I can pull her inside."

In less than five minutes, the camp had been broken, teams were hitched and all was in readiness. Everets looked everything over, then walked to where Lucifer remained picketed. He slipped a bridle over the big gelding's head and led him to the wagons.

"We'll take him along. He'll fetch a good price, I'll wager."

"You bastard," Zelda hissed quietly, still nursing her sore cheek.

Chapter Five

Movement came through at the first coherent awareness. The rumble, creak and squeak of a wagon in motion clearly formed in her mind. Why couldn't she see? Charity Rose pondered the question a moment. Then her awakening senses informed her that something, a blanket or cloth, had been placed over her face. Now a new question arose. Why couldn't she move? Within seconds she realized she had been bound hand and foot. A prisoner? Of whom? And why? The cloth rustled, jerked away, and light stabbed at her eyes.

"You're awake," Charlie Cramer said in a soft voice. "Here, let me take that off your mouth."

Charity's throat burned, and she croaked when she attempted to speak. "Wha—where, ah . . ."

Charlie extended a half-filled cup of water. Charity drank from it greedily. She wet her lips and tried again.

"Where are we? What happened?"

Eyes downcast, Charlie explained in a chastened tone. "It's all Lane's doing. He—he wants you to work with us. So he put something in your coffee to knock you out. We're headed toward Campo. That's in Colorado."

That explained a lot. Particularly the tight bonds. Charity tugged against them once more. "Can . . . can you let me go? Loosen these? They hurt."

"I—I'm not supposed to. Lane'd beat me if something happened and you got away."

"I . . . I won't try to run. I promise," Charity answered. "Only my fingers and toes are numb. Please, Charlie. At least loosen the ropes a little."

"All right. Just a little, though. And, I brought you something to eat. It's near to sunup, but Lane don't want to stop. Not till we get to Campo."

"Why did he do this? I know you said he wanted to put me to work with you girls, but why?"

"He says you'll make more money than any two of us. You've got a fresh, new look, he calls it. It'll all work out, you'll see. After a couple of towns, you won't have to be tied up all the time."

"What he's doing is against the law," Charity protested. "Don't you see that? Lane has abducted me. That's a crime. He can't just make me become a . . . a working girl," Charity insisted, softening her remark abruptly in deference to the sweet-faced young woman who aided her.

Charlie gave her a blank expression. "What's to stop him from it? He's our *man*. He's in charge of us. He looks out for us, provides us with food, a place to live and to work. He even gives us some cash money from time to time to spend as we wish."

"How very generous of him," Charity said dryly. "Can't you see that you're prisoners, just like me? You may not have any ropes on, but you're not free, either."

Charlie blushed slightly. "He lets us do what . . . I like the best. What advantage would I have on my own? Don't you see, Charity? He takes care of us. He's our protector."

Realizing she could not pierce this twisted logic all at once, Charity changed the subject. "What about Lucifer?

My packhorse? What about them and Butch?"

"Lucifer's tied on the tailgate of this wagon; so's your packhorse," Charlie answered, and then tears welled in her eyes. "L-Lane sh-shot your dog. It's—it's the meanest thing I ever saw him do."

"*Shot him!* Oh, no, no. Oh, Butch." Unable to contain her grief, Charity wept freely. Tied and helpless, without Butch, what could she hope to do? Heartsick, she sobbed in wretched misery as desolation settled on her.

"We're well on our way, Otto," Karl Richter gloated in his law office in Cottonwood Springs, Kansas. "I've sent the petition off to the state capital to have Cottonwood Springs recognized as the county seat. The Supreme Court should rule on it within two weeks. Then we can make our move."

"Are you sure ve can get away vit it?" Otto inquired, nervous.

"Of course we can. In the squabbles back and forth, some of the records got lost is all. We tell it that way and stick to it, who is to question? We'll take over a few homesteads at a time, not get greedy. We simply fill in fictitious names and evict the people on a farm here, one there, another over Hopewell way. Then we let a few months go by and do it again. In some cases we can wait until someone dies off. Then, when their estate is probated, we step in with the claim to the land. Before long we'll be rich beyond belief."

"Von't they fight it?" Otto inquired.

"How can they? There's no recorded deed. Nothing to prove their claim and everything to prove ours. I'll simply be working for a client back East who purchased the property and had it registered. A little judicious backdating and some money spread in the proper places will insure we win."

Outside, storm clouds blackened the sky. Huge anvil-topped thunderheads swelled thousands of feet into the air. Lightning flickered, and the ominous rumble that announced a Kansas deluge rolled over the red-brown soil. Otto Blutcher rose to light a lamp. He'd taken only a step when the outer door slammed open and three armed men crowded into the room.

"What is this?" Karl Richter demanded.

"Shut up," a masked individual growled.

Two more men, their faces hidden behind bandanas, shoved in and began rummaging through stacks of books and journals. When they located what they sought, they started stuffing the objects into gunnysacks.

"You can't do that," Richter protested in a strangled voice.

It immediately earned him a cold, hard steel muzzle in his throat. Eyes wide and wild, Karl Richter looked down at the cocked six-gun and attempted to swallow around the painful pressure it made against his larynx. All of the intruders went to work then, filling bags with the county ledgers and records. One ripped open the drawers of Richter's desk, dumping the contents onto the floor until he located the county seals. Satisfied, they started for the door. Karl Richter saw his bold plans escaping with them and made a courageous, if foolish, move.

His hand barely touched the forestock of the Winchester that leaned in a corner by his desk when a bullet smashed through his arm. Karl slammed back against his swivel chair and howled in agony. As the raiders hurried out, he tightly clutched the profusely bleeding wound.

"Do something, dammit," he managed in a pain-filled voice. "They're getting away with the county seat!"

Curious, anticipating a substantial feed, three large black vultures descended in lazy spirals toward the unmoving object below. The persistent breeze ruffled the gray-black fur, giving a semblance of life that startled the buzzards away for a moment. When no other movement followed in a patient ten minutes of circling, they dropped lower, large flat feet extended to meet the earth. One settled ungracefully onto the ground some five feet from their intended meal.

Waddling like a drunken sailor, wings spread for balance, the carrion-eating creature advanced, appetite controlling its dim brain. The weak whine that came from the object of its desire surprised the vulture. It squawked raucously and stumbled backward. Extending its long, scrawny, scarlet-hued neck, it croaked encouragement to the others. Wary, its companions joined it in stalking their breakfast. An almost ritual dance began, with first one, then another of the awkward birds advancing in a sort of controlled fall, then leaping back a step or two. Another whine came, and the trio squawked loudly and made bumbling attempts to lift quickly into the air.

One moved a bit too slowly as gray fur flashed below them. Steel-trap jaws snapped closed on a leg, and the vulture flapped uselessly as its would-be meal became its conqueror. Pain in his neck wound caused Butch to release the bird before he could vanquish it. Crying in terror and agony, it ponderously gained the sky and joined its companions in escape. They would seek some less menacing prey.

On the ground, Butch shivered with weakness. The bullet had passed through the loose flesh at the scruff of his neck. He'd bled considerably and the wound had suppurated. Fortunately the muscles had not been damaged. He felt the terrible need of hunger, a weakness every bit as dangerous as the infected bullet hole. Straining against the hurt, Butch turned his head until he could lick feebly at the break in his flesh. Time passed while he rested and cleaned away the oozing pus.

Sunlight lay warmly on his thick pelt. It loosened tightened muscles, and the partly feral canine tried to make sense of the impressions that flitted through his brain. It had been the dark time when he had been hurt. He recalled his mistress and sensed danger to her. Weakly Butch rose and walked a few unsteady feet toward the bank of a shallow creek. He ended his trek on his belly, barely able to pull himself along the rough ground. At last his tongue touched water. He lapped at it and felt quickening energy within his flagging body. Slowly he eased his way further into the stream.

Darkness came again, and he remained half in the water. The chill liquid washed away at his wound. Slowly he sensed renewed vigor in his muscular torso and powerful legs. With a grunt and whine, he came upright. Some ten feet away a small rabbit froze in panic, a black silhouette in the moonlight. Butch swayed unsteadily, then leaped toward his prey.

A scrabble of claws on the caliche and the rabbit died with a tiny squeal. Butch disemboweled his catch and feasted. He could almost feel the strength flowing warmly through his abused body. Contented for the time being, he slept until daylight. As he woke, movement revealed a small raccoon on a bank not far from him. He gathered his legs and bunched muscles. In a single leap, he landed on the furry little animal. Butch crunched his jaws on the skull before the vicious creature could use its own teeth to advantage.

Again he fed, and the strength flowed richer through him. Once more he licked at his wound. The pus had stopped flowing, but a dull, throbbing pain remained. Visions returned dimly to his animal brain. He began sniffing the ground and located a familiar odor.

His big, black, hoofed friend had been here. Butch could still make out the direction the horse had taken. He smelled his mistress, too. A great longing filled him. Still a bit unsteady, he started off along the invisible trail of Lucifer's scent.

Nightfall found the mobile cathouse only twenty-five miles from its destination. Charity Rose remained bound in the wagon. Charlie had become her regular caretaker. She came with food and a tin cup of weak tea. Charity groaned as she tried to sit upright.

"If you'll . . . promise not to do anything, I'll untie your hands so you can eat proper-like," Charlie offered.

"I'd appreciate that, Charlie. I—I seem to hurt everywhere. I know I've asked a dozen times, but I still can't see why he's doing this to me."

"For the money, of course. Lane takes good care of us and that costs a lot. Relax, Charity. Don't get yourself all upset. You'll like it after a while, I know you will. We haven't any worries and Lane sees we have time for being alone when we need it."

Charlie's simplistic view and the innocence with which she delivered it touched Charity's heart. Yet she knew that under this guise of "taking care of them" something malignant lurked in Lane Everets. No matter that, Charity thought defiantly; the first town they came to, she'd be able to break away, get to the law and get protection.

She was not some girl with no past and no family. If necessary a telegraph message to Mark McDade at Doz Cabezas, or to Aunt Megan, Padre Gomez or any number of persons would substantiate her story. Lane Everets had no claim on her. Thinking it eased her trepidation.

Charlie might have been reading her thoughts from what she said next. "Ever' new girl we get, Lane breaks them in when we first get to a town. After that . . . they don't want to go anywhere else. You'll see."

"What do you mean, *'breaks them in'?*"

"Well, ah, he, ah, has us do, things. Do things with

50

him that no one would want to be known they, ah, did. Sometimes he has to hit a girl to keep her in line. But they all turn out loving him in the end. You'll see."

That simple assurance, repeated with nearly each frightening revelation, did more to unsettle Charity than the unseen menace of Lane Everets, only a few feet away.

Chapter Six

Mark McDade sat in his office in Dos Cabezas, reading a copy of the El Paso newspaper. It contained an account of the Wilkes-Carroll feud. In it, he could clearly see the involvement of Charity Rose. Bright sunlight and searing desert heat failed to penetrate the cool shadows of the thick-walled adobe jail and sheriff's office, for which Mark was duly and properly grateful.

He'd returned the previous afternoon from a long, roundabout chase that had netted two frightened Mexican youths in their mid-teens. They had taken some unbranded calves, unaware of the law governing ownership based on a cow and its calf. By the time the story had reached Mark's office, it had been blown into a full-scale rustling operation. When he had at last encountered the youngsters, their sincere contrition and obvious confusion over the finer points of law convinced Mark that they had no criminal intent. All the same, he brought them back — if for no other reason than that he needed help herding the fractious calves.

Once the missing stock had been returned and an explanation given, Mark rode on into Dos Cabezas. After a good night's sleep and a hearty breakfast, he settled down with the paper, and his thoughts immediately turned to Charity Rose. The tone of the article indicated that the feud had ended, primarily through the efforts of a Bob Carroll and a Miss Charity Rose. If so, where was she now?

Mark had no illusions about Charity. They were good friends and nothing more. He still felt discomfort over the manner in which she had left Dos Cabezas with the Uzzels, a family of itinerant missionaries, after an unpleasant scene with Tom Thornton. That had been months ago. Since then, Tom had avoided speaking with Mark, and the young sheriff had no words to explain the situation. Was that what kept Charity away from home? With the feud ended, she should be back by now. As though privy to the workings of his mind, Megan Quincannon opened the door and entered.

"G'dmarnin' to ye, Mark," the stout spinster boomed. "I've come to inquire, have ye heard anything from me niece, Charity?"

"Miss Megan, you know if I had any news, you'd be the first to know. I do have five days' mail here unopened. Let me sort through that and we might learn something."

"Sure, that's an idea, it is. While ye do, I'll be fixin' a fit cup o' tea far ye. I brought along some of those sweet rolls ye like so much," she added with a wink.

"You're not trying to bribe me, are you, Miss Megan?"

"Perish the thought! It's only a kindness, it is."

Mark began opening mail. The fifth letter down was a yellow envelope from the telegraph office in Wilcox. He opened it and exclaimed happily.

"Listen to this. A request from the Harrison County, Texas, sheriff to verify bounty on three members of the Concho Bill Baudine gang. Bounty to be paid to C. M. Rose. This is dated, ah . . . five days ago. We know she was well and still in Longview as of then. Could be she's on her way home now."

"By all the saints, I hope so," Megan responded, her ample bosom aquiver with concern. "The poor darlin's suffered enough. There's not any more misery should be comin' her way."

The skyline of Campo, Colorado, consisted of a truncated, tin-sided gristmill, half a dozen brick and clapboard buildings in the business district and a few scattered houses on side streets. Nearly more populous than dwellings and businesses were the outhouses. Many establishments sported no less than two—one for men and one for women—and often a third or fourth. It had prompted one wag to suggest that the people of Campo were full of shit.

That witticism had been delivered shortly before its author was escorted out of town, properly tarred and feathered, hanging from a rail upside down. Not that the citizens of Campo took inordinate pride in their community; rather, they took umbrage at being described in such earthy terms. From a cursory examination of the commercial center of Campo, one would gather that the occupation of the residents revolved solely around the consumption of alcoholic beverages and the pursuit of other vices.

Three saloons, the Rocky Mountain Casino, and two dance halls, Nell Forbisher's being the more notorious of them, graced the two-block hub of the village, with the usual general mercantile, blacksmith and livery, saddle-and-harness shop and gristmill. All that with a population of 278. Campo sizzled under a hot midday sun when the odd caravan of traveling bawds rolled into town and halted behind Nell Forbisher's.

"You Everets?" a gaunt, drawn woman of forty or so demanded from the stoop.

"I am," Lane Everets responded.

"About time you got here. All my girls have either run off or got married. I'm in a hell of a fix. C'mon in an' we'll talk terms."

"Not much to talk about. I got the girls. You want to use them, it'll be by my say-so. Keeps it plain and simple that way."

Nell Forbisher angrily tossed her stiff, brass red-dyed curls, small hands on her hips, and glowered at Lane Everets. "You wouldn't be fixin' to take advantage of a woman with the hurts, would you?" she demanded, eyes squinted.

"Not if I didn't figure I could get away with it," Everets informed her good-naturedly. "Zelda, you get the girls settled in while Miss Nell and I talk business."

In Nell's office, done with lots of lace, chintz and powder blue, Nell put on a pair of gold-rimmed spectacles and poured whiskey from a crystal decanter, then handed a glass to Lane. They took seats and Nell sipped deeply, lips smacking in appreciation, before conversation began. The madam had her own plan, and Everets' statement to the contrary had hardly fazed her.

"I'll provide room, board and everything they need. I want sixty percent right off the top and you provide the girls' share out of your part."

"Apparently it ain't just your eyesight that's failin'," Lane countered. "I said we'd do this according to *my* terms. The way I see that sixty-forty split is the other way around."

"*I've* got the place, sonny boy, *and* the customers. What else you reckon to do? You gonna sell 'em out the back of your wagons?"

A smug smirk illuminated Everets' face. "It's been done before. The thing is, you ain't got any girls and I do. They can work anywhere, even on a haystack. You'd be wise to accept my proposition."

Nell's eyes glittered like agates behind the thick lenses. Her thin mouth puckered in concentration, and the lines that denoted her years in the oldest profession deepened to crevasses. She disliked any form of bickering. She disliked most of all being put on the spot by a man. Yet, he had a point.

"Well, ah, perhaps we could compromise?" Nell offered, when a loud knock interrupted. "What is it?" she demanded.

Zelda's voice came from outside. "It's the new girl, Lane," she responded. "Somehow she's gotten loose of her bonds and she's fightin' like a wildcat."

"Dammit!" Lane exploded, then realized his tactical error.

"I don't take any girls in who aren't where they want to be," Nell told Lane coldly. "Can't abide anyone yellin' to the law."

"She'll be right as rain in a day or so. Brand new to the business is all. Once I, ah, break her in," Lane hastened to explain, "she'll be meek as a lamb."

"You had best see to it," Nell ground out.

"I'll do it right now," Lane offered, rising.

"No. We deal first, you do that later. Say, fifty-fifty?"

Lane looked hard at Nell, pretending to have to weigh the offer. The sixty-forty split she'd first proposed had been generous enough. Lane's innate greed had demanded he seek better terms. Now he made a show of relenting with ill grace.

"You're thievin' me, and you know it, Nell. Hell, just because I got a fractious girl to knock in line don't mean . . ."

"It means I got you over a barrel, is what," Nell snapped back. "Is it a deal?"

"Dammit, I could go broke that way," Lane grumbled. "All right, Nell. Deal."

"Good. Now go take care of your mustang filly."

Lane Everets found Charity Rose struggling in the back of the wagon, with four girls holding her down. He climbed over the tailgate and gave Charity a vicious backhand slap that crimsoned her cheek. She stiffened, and hatred poured from her eyes.

"You can't hold me like this and you know it," Charity hissed. "I'll fix you good, you son of a bitch."

Lane laughed. His thick, sensual lips curled in a sneer. "Little bit of a thing like you? What could you ever do?" he taunted.

"In the last two years," Charity told him coldly, "I've killed over seventeen men. Two of them were Apaches. On the first day of May, a year ago, I gunned down Big Ed Detrich at the O.K. Corral in Tombstone. You've heard of him?"

Such a bland pronouncement stunned Everets. He'd heard of Ed Detrich's death at the hands of a bounty hunter, yet even now could not connect this feisty young woman with the deed.

"Everyone's heard of Big Ed. Way I hear it, he got taken by a young bounty hunter."

"You see the way I'm dressed," Charity said simply. "Before I'm finished, I'm going to collect the price on every member of the Baudine gang. Now let me out of here."

"Oh, no. That's where you're wrong, missy. I got an investment in you. You're gonna stand up and come along nice-like, or I'll do it the hard way."

Charity started to struggle and Lane hit her again. The girls sprang out of the way, and although staggered by the blow, Charity lashed out with her nails, raking Lane's cheeks.

"You bitch!" he wailed.

Careful not to mar her delicate features, Everets went to work on Charity's vulnerable belly. Pain exploded inside her and she fought back in whatever manner she could. Everets dragged her from the wagon, and she flailed with both arms. A solid connection with her left fist made his ear ring. She raised a booted heel into his crotch and he groaned. Doubled over, he still managed to rush her through the back door.

They sprawled on the rear staircase. Charity bit him in one shoulder. Everets howled at the fiery teeth wounds and slammed a fist into one of Charity's kidneys. Breath exploded from her. Dizzy and weakened, she gave little resistance until they reached the second-floor landing. There she rammed an elbow into Lane's chest and broke free.

Charity managed to run several steps before the enraged pimp caught up to her. Her mannish jacket ripped in his viselike grip, and her shirt came after. Lane whirled her around and yanked down the restraining band that disguised her breasts. The pink-tipped mounds burst free. In a furor of her own, Charity punched Lane in the mouth.

His lip split and blood ran freely. Using a balled fist, he thumped her with all his strength atop the head. For a moment Charity's eyes crossed, then rolled up. As she slumped, Everets caught her and carried her to a room at the far end of the hall. There he dumped her on the bed and lashed her tightly to the head- and footrails. Then he stalked to the door.

"I'll be back to break you in later," he threatened. Then the sensual sight before him commanded his full attention. "Nice tits. You'll make a lot of money, baby."

Lane Everets slammed and locked the door, then stalked down the hall. Eyes wide, his girls stared at the cuts, scrapes and broken skin that testified to his difficulty in subduing Charity Rose. They'd never, they agreed after his scowling departure, seen anything like it.

Because he was alone and hurt, Butch's wolf instincts came to the fore. He traveled mostly at night and avoided contact with humans. When his stomach demanded it, he stalked game and took it, while still faithfully following the scent of his friends. His ribs began to grow gaunt, and his coat lost its usual healthy luster. Still he would not abandon the quest in favor of the relative comfort and ease of the wild life. Somewhere ahead, he dimly sensed, his help was needed.

Three days passed in such a manner, drawing him always westward. When he could, he located water and bathed his wound. Slowly his strength returned. It flowed like rich, warm sap through his veins, heating the muscles, removing stiffness. By the fourth day, Butch no longer trotted along with his tail tucked protectively and submissively between his legs. Briskly upright, like a furry flag, it curved rakishly over his back. His eyes shone brightly, no longer clouded with mucus. In the distance, he could make out the shapes of a man place.

Closer in, Butch's feral instincts and racial memory told him that the irregular collection of shapes on the horizon represented danger to him. Yet another part of his mind summoned him on, keeping bright his sense of duty to his mistress and the horse. Nighttime found him on his belly, no more than fifty yards outside the east end of town. The scent trail he'd followed seemed stronger here, despite the many conflicting ones he encountered.

With the coming of full darkness, Butch slipped quietly into town. On soft footpads he negotiated the twisting way between buildings, clinging to the distinctive odor he associated with his friends. It grew stronger as he progressed toward a tall building, brightly lit, where the noise of people and raucous music came from within. There, at the rear, the scent disappeared.

Puzzled, Butch made a complete circuit of the loud place, returning at last to the rear, where he waited quietly on his haunches. Before long a door banged open and a man staggered out onto the stoop. He swayed, thrust his head left and right, then moved erratically out into the yard and bent far over. Strangling sounds came from him as he voided the vile contents of his stomach onto the parched earth.

Without wasting a moment to consider, Butch sprang upright and dashed into the place.

Chapter Seven

Turned low to the point of guttering, a kerosene lamp provided a sickly yellow light in the room upstairs at Nell Forbisher's dance hall. The small cubicle contained a bed, a washstand, a chamber pot and the lamp. Charity Rose lay naked and spread-eagled on the bed, hands bound to the cast-iron headposts, ankles securely tied to the footrails. Even in the dim illumination, her body glistened with a fine film of perspiration. It represented fear, not passion, generated by the ordeal she underwent at the hands of Lane Everets.

Everets, likewise naked, stood over her, the bunched muscles of his lean body rippling as he changed position, selecting a new place to bring hurt. On one hand he wore a thin leather glove; the other held a lighted cigar.

"I haven't burnt you yet, but I might, if you don't cooperate. I don't know why you're still resisting. Any woman who goes around masquerading as a man is asking for it. You love it, don't you? Well, when I get through you'll take it any way you can get it. I'm gonna probe every opening of your body until you beg for mercy. You're gonna get down off that high-minded pillar you're livin' on and come face-to-face with what you really are. Then . . . then you'll do anything you can to make daddy happy. You'll see."

Oh God, the same mindless phrase Charlie Cramer repeated so blankly, Charity thought with renewed fear. She'd endured rape before, could do so again, she believed, without losing her mind. Yet the indignities Everets promised her caused revulsion to rise from her stomach. Sour bile burned in her throat. Despite her determination to remain unmoved by his brutalities, when Everets climbed onto the bed, Charity screamed.

"What's that dog doing up here?" Nell Forbisher's voice demanded.

"It—it looks like the one Char—" Charlene Cramer began when Charity's screams came from the room at the far end of the hall.

Instantly, Butch launched himself at the thin wooden panel that served as a door. The cheap latch gave under his weight, and Butch's claws scrabbled on the floor as he streaked unerringly toward the bed. Lips peeled back to expose white fangs, he didn't bother with a warning growl. A final leap and the screams coming from the room changed to howls of masculine pain.

Sharp teeth sunk in Lane Everets' shoulder, Butch sought purchase on the bed linen as he yanked his victim right and left. Attacked from behind, Everets struggled feebly to dislodge the furry fury that clung to him. Blood ran in scarlet rivulets over his pasty white skin. For a flashing second, Butch released him, and he managed to turn part way before the fangs ripped into his right pectoral muscle and began to shred flesh.

Wailing and shrieking for help, Everets fell onto his side, legs quivering while Butch straddled him and continued to savage bare flesh. "Make him stop!" the vicious pimp begged. "Make him let me go! Oh, please, help me!"

Zelda Parker and Charlene Cramer gathered courage enough to enter. They, too, implored Charity to call off the ravening animal. Through it all, Charity remained silent. Zelda knelt beside the bed, close to Charity's face.

"Please, honey, please stop your dog. He's—he's killin' Lane."

"Get something to tie Lane up and I'll call Butch off," Charity answered.

"Oh, we couldn't do that," Zelda responded. "Lane's our man, you see. He'd never forgive us if we tied him up."

"Then cut me loose. I won't call Butch off unless I'm free."

With nervous mien, the two soiled doves consulted each other. A nod from Charlene put them both in action. One worked on Charity's hands, the other her feet. In no time they had the bonds loosened. Charity pulled herself from under the writhing, howling Everets and found a cheap dressing gown on a peg fitted into the wall. She wrapped herself in this, then turned, almost casually, toward the bed.

"Amach, Butch. *Amach."*

At the command in Gaelic, Butch instantly ceased his savaging of Everets' flesh and assumed a guard position at the head of the bed. The hall and doorway had filled with frightened, curious hookers. In the pile of Lane's clothing, Charity found a small pistol and cocked it. She stepped close to the huddled, sobbing form and shoved the cold steel muzzle against the side of his head.

"Get up, you son of a bitch. I ought to shoot off your balls for this," Charity hotly threw at him. "As it is, I'm going to take you in on a charge of abduction and forced servitude. That means slavery, in case you don't know the word. You'll be getting out of jail around time to celebrate your fiftieth birthday." She turned to the women, as though seeing them for the first time.

"You," Charity commanded Nell Forbisher. "Get my clothes and bring them here. My guns, too. Any foolishness and I'll splatter his brains all over your pretty room."

While she waited, she commanded Everets, "Get up and get dressed. You're headed for the marshal's office."

"D-don't take me there," Everets pleaded. "There's a—a flier out on me from Texas. I—I—I'll do anything, pay anything you ask, just don't turn me in to the law."

"Well, I make a little profit for my suffering, eh?" Charity goaded him.

"Wha-what do you mean?" Everets inquired, trying to staunch the bleeding from his chest with a towel from the washstand.

"You should have asked me what I did for a living, instead of assuming I was a whore. I'm a bounty hunter, Lane Everets, and I'm going to take great pleasure collecting on you."

Black smoke poured from the tall diamond stack of the AT&SF locomotive pulling Local No. 9 from Newton to Dodge City. The big drivers turned with hypnotic rhythm, and steam belched from glands and valves all over the big 4-6-2 Baldwin. Black paint and brass shone everywhere. Back in the passenger cars, a holiday atmosphere prevailed. Particularly for Bobby Pritchard.

Bobby, along with his parents and two sisters, was on his way to Dodge to celebrate his eleventh birthday at his grandparents' home. Big, liquid brown eyes peered widely from under the mop of his nearly white blond bangs as he stared out over the flat countryside. Western Kansas was nothing like their hilly home in Lecompton. The slender lad grew quite agitated when he saw six men streaking across the tablelike prairie at an angle to intersect the track at some distance ahead.

"Oh, look, Momma. They want to race the train!" Bobby shouted.

"Yes, son," his mother responded, patting her child's head.

Like a shot, Bobby came out of his seat and ran down the aisle. "It's a race! It's a race!"

Out on the vestibule he found six more men approaching from the other side. While Bobby stared at them in consternation, they raised bandanas over their faces and drew six-guns. All at once the realization struck him. Scrambling back inside, he bellowed his discovery at full lung power.

"It's Jesse James, Momma! It's Jesse James!"

"Wha—?"

"What's that?" raised, anxious voices echoed.

"They're gonna stick up the tra-ain! They're gonna stick up the tra-ain!" Bobby informed the startled passengers in a singsong voice.

Almost on top of this intelligence, the nine-car local began to slow perceptibly. A thicker billow came from the smokestack, and the wheels began to shriek on the rails. A long, frozen moment passed; then the front door to the car flew open and two men entered, faces masked by colorful bandanas, ready six-guns menacing everyone.

"Howdy folks, we come to lighten your burdens a bit. Don't no one try to be a hero. My friend here will pass among you with a bag. Kindly remove all your valuables and deposit them inside it. Don't be stinting and don't try to deceive us. We aim to get it all."

"Now, see here, young man," a portly man in an expensive suit blustered. "I'm an officer of this line.

You'll not get away with this. We'll have the Pinkertons on you before you've ridden a mile."

"Mister, I eat Pinks for breakfast and spit out tin badges. If you won't want a forty-five-sized decoration between your eyes, I'd suggest you sit down and do as you're told."

A third man, better dressed than the other outlaws, appeared in the open doorway. Even with his face masked, Bobby could tell he was smiling. "Everything seems to be going well here," Concho Bill Baudine remarked. "Speed it up a little, boys. We're going to have to dynamite the express car."

"A-are you Jesse James?" Bobby asked, big-eyed, his face radiating awe.

"No, son, I ain't. But you can tell your kids, when you get old enough to have 'em, that you got robbed by Concho Bill Baudine."

"Goll-lee! M-Mr. Baudine, ah, please, it's my birthday an' please don't take along my presents? Please?"

Concho Bill reached out and ruffled Bobby's fine, pale blonde hair. "Why, I'd never think of such a thing. Don't you worry, boy."

"M'name's Bobby. Bobby Pritchard," the child piped. "An', ah, thank you, Mister Baudine."

"You're welcome, Bobby. Boys," Baudine went on, raising his voice. "You heard what the kid said. Anything you find wrapped like a present, don't take it."

Excited to the point of babbling, Bobby turned to hug his mother's arm. "Gosh, he's—he's *wonderful*."

For the life of him, Bobby could never figure out why his mother sat there quietly crying.

Blue jays scolded the robins who searched the dew-wet grass for worms. Worried mother quail whistled for their wayward broods. A soft morning breeze had come up, rustling the saw-edged, spade-shaped leaves of the cottonwoods. Charity Rose awoke exhilarated by the wonderful feel of freedom. She stretched and breathed deeply, arose and bathed her face and arms in a large glazed crockery basin. She dressed with the happy knowledge that she had become five hundred dollars richer from the capture of Lane Everets. Her gear all packed, she descended to the lobby of the small hotel in Campo and asked that a boy take her things to the livery. Then she entered the small alcove that served as a dining area.

She was enjoying a light breakfast when the first of the soiled doves came to her. Charlene Cramer was red-eyed from weeping, as was Penelope Saunders. They wrung their hands and spoke imploringly.

"What are we to do now?" Charlene wailed. "We're all alone. How can we—can we ever get work?"

"You're a grown woman, you can take care of yourself," Charity told her, her recent ordeal too vivid to allow her much compassion.

"B-but Lane always did for us," Penelope protested. "Without him, we're lost."

"No you're not!" Charity snapped.

"They're right," Zelda Parker said emphatically as she joined the others. "With Lane in jail, we have no one to arrange our travel plans and set up locations to work."

"You must be capable of doing something besides . . . besides what you've been doing," Charity countered.

"Honey, that's *all* we've ever done," Zelda replied.

"It's true," sobbed little Tina Lewis, youngest of the soiled doves at barely fifteen. "I never even learned to cook or sew before I got turned out by my uncle and that woman he married."

Of all of them, Tina's circumstance most affected Charity. "Oh, Tina, when was that?"

"Three years ago," Tina answered blankly. "I hadn't but barely turned twelve."

"That's *awful*," Charity flared, her temper rising at people so callous as to enslave a mere child to serving the lusts of indifferent men. "But . . . what can I do about it? How can I help?"

"You got rid of Lane," Tina urged. "I never liked him anyway. He was mean. He's gone and you're here in his place." The matter seemed simple and solved to her.

"I won't be here long. I've leaving this morning for Kansas."

"We can go along!" Zelda and two others chorused.

"Th-that's impossible," Charity stammered.

"No, it's not. You're our new master. Where you go, we go," Tina told her.

Loath to take on any such responsibility, repelled by the implication of assuming any authority over these terribly young ladies of the evening, Charity summoned all her wits to make a reasonable argument. The longer she talked, the more she sensed she had already failed. By then all nine girls hovered around her table, and she received distinctly nasty looks from the proprietress. Exasperated, her last arguments exhausted, she struck upon a compromise.

"All right, girls. I'll tell you what we can do."

"Yes?" rippled eagerly from one soiled dove to another.

"I'll . . . I'll see you all safely to Kansas. There I'm sure you can find new, respectable jobs. Maybe we can even find someone to take Tina in, let her finish her schooling."

"I'm too old for that," Tina said wistfully. "I want to work."

"Then we'll find you something fun and interesting to do," Charity promised.

"Will it . . . will it be a nice, new saloon?" Tina asked

in a small voice.

Groaning in resignation, Charity made ready to leave. There would be a lot of packing and preparing to do before they started out for Kansas.

Chapter Eight

Startled birds rose in squawking protest as glass shattered in a window of the Crowley County courthouse in Hopewell, Kansas. The bullet that punched through the pane whipped across Main Street and embedded in the front of Jeremy Bittles' general mercantile. The loud thump that announced its arrival sent the round-faced, pudgy-handed mayor of Hopewell sputtering around his counter, six-gun in hand.

"B-by dammit, they're after the records again!" he shouted to everyone in general as he headed for the door. His pince-nez popped from his button nose.

Loud thumps, shouts and the crack of another gunshot came from inside the courthouse. More glass broke, and Hiram Weeks, the county clerk, came staggering out the door, clutching his belly.

"They shot me," Weeks said in a wondering tone. "They shot me, Jeremy."

"I'll get the marshal," Bittles responded, urging his rotund body into agitated motion in the direction of the marshal's office.

Four men, their faces concealed behind flour-sack hoods, emerged from the county seat, their arms loaded with ledgers and record books. These they deposited in the bed of a buckboard driven by another hooded raider, who had a bandaged right arm. The driver slapped the reins on his team's rumps and the rig moved off at a good clip. Their task completed, the remaining raiders made for their horses as gunshots sounded from down the street.

"Hold on now," Sheriff Orin Meadows called out to the angry men of Hopewell as they started for their mounts. "No sense in chasin' after them when we can use our heads and catch 'em easy."

"How's that, Sheriff?" Jeremy Bittles demanded, anxious to go after the villains who had again stolen the county seat.

"Since we know where they're goin', we let Marshal Tuttle and a few men pursue them, keep them running hard. They'll try to throw us off by headin' elsewhere. When their critters wear down you can be sure they'll slow the pace. While that's goin' on, we cut around and ambush them."

His idea caught on at once. Ben Tuttle, the marshal, raised a hand over his head for attention. "I want four men to come with me. The rest will go with the sheriff."

Sheriff Meadows' plan worked to perfection. Horses could only maintain a gallop for so long before tiring to the point of collapse. Once the pursuit slowed, the group with the county lawman bypassed the fleeing band from Cottonwood Springs and located themselves in a cluster of rocks that spanned the main road, some three miles outside the rival town. There they waited.

Karl Richter drove the wagon, his confidence high after the ease with which they had liberated the records. Even the damned posse chasing them had played out and lagged far behind. Only occasionally did he see puffs of dust that indicated they continued the pursuit. They'd not catch up and they'd be met with a hot enough reception if they ventured into Cottonwood Springs. Karl had about decided to throw a party for his friends that evening when his hat suddenly took flight from his head.

"Hot damn! What's that?" he bellowed excitedly in the instant before he heard the report of the rifle. Then he turned back toward his companions and shouted, "Ambush!"

More weapons opened up among the rocks ahead, puffs of smoke betraying their location. Richter felt trapped on the exposed seat of the wagon, yet he feared for his life if he stood up to dismount. A bullet slapped into the mudguard and he opted for an ungainly dive over the side. He hit hard and rolled, to come up cursing when he realized he'd not set the brake.

Unrestrained, the frightened horses bolted forward and ran wildly down the road. Bawling hoarsely, Richter started after them. His companions had enough to trouble them, exchanging shots with the ambushers. How had they managed it? Richter could see no reasonable way to explain the surprise attack. Could it be a third town, seeking to seize the county seat for themselves?

"Pour it on, boys," Sheriff Meadows shouted over the crash of gunshots. "We want them to know right certain they can't get away with something like that."

Luther Thorne, the banker in Hopewell, took careful aim with his Winchester and squeezed off a round. The curved metal butt plate slammed satisfyingly into his shoulder, and past the smoke he saw a horse rear and throw its rider.

"They got Mort in the shoulder," Ruben Fenn shouted to Dallas Avery. "We better pull outta here."

"Karl's wagon," Dallas called back. "It's runnin' loose."

"Forget that. We could get ourselves killed out here," Ruben complained.

"You goin' yellow, Ruben?" Josh Harper accused.

"Hell no, Josh, I just got good sense."

Harper snorted derisively a moment before a hot slug punched through the insubstantial cloth of his whipcord trousers and cut a fiery, blood-welling gouge in his left leg. Eyes wide and white, he touched his right spur to his mount's ribs and galloped away at right angles to the ambush.

"Looks like Josh's got the same idea," Ruben observed. "Help me with Mort and let's get the hell outta here."

Up in the rocks, Sheriff Meadows spotted the runaway wagon and pointed it out to his small posse. "Looks like the county seat is comin' back to us with no trouble. Emil, you and Clyde get down there and stop that wagon," he told Emil Taller and Clyde Noonan.

"Sure enough, Sheriff," Emil agreed.

With the Cottonwood Springs men fleeing and the wagon all but under control, the shooting stopped. The Hopewell men raised a small cheer and popped up among the rocks. They retrieved their horses and surrounded the wagon as Emil Taller climbed aboard and took the reins. The records would go safely back to Hopewell.

Grover Dalton wiped sweat-caked dust from his face, leaving a white streak across his eyes like a reversal of the mask of a raccoon. Nine thousand prime beef, headed up the trail to Dodge City like the old days. There hadn't been a trail herd since the railroad came to West Texas. Then tick fever had brought an end to the northern cattle drives, for all save a few who had it set in their minds to take cattle to Montana or Wyoming, such like. Grover Dalton had been a kid of twelve on his first drive to Elsworth back in '69. Now he was trail boss of his own herd, taking it north for nostalgia's sake as much as anything else. The damned Jayhawkers were liable to stop him with a quarantine anyway, if they got word of his coming.

He had a good crew, one he could trust to push the cows through, failing anything but a shutdown by money-hungry bandits in Kansas pretending to represent the state government. Damned Jayhawkers. His father had fought them and so had Grover. There was just enough truth in the Texas tick-fever scare to put sympathy on the side of the former followers of that damned abolitionist, John Brown. The Texicans had lost and the Kansas market dried up. Grover's contemporaries had laughed at him when he suggested a trail drive. After all, tick fever had not been around to plague the herds in eight years now. His animals were healthy, he knew that. Well, they'd reach the Kansas line in three days; then he'd know if the legalized thieves were laying for him or not. In the meantime, he had a lot more to do.

"Hey, Petey," Grover called to the youngest of his drovers. "Time to come off drag for a while. Get yourself some water from the chuck wagon barrel and help Cookie set up for supper."

Grinning, the lean, lanky, blond-haired youngster waved to his boss. "Yes, sir, Mister Dalton. Be a pleasure to quit eatin' dust." The kid touched spurs to his mount as he cut away from the rear of the herd and loped along the left side, headed for the chuck wagon, far ahead.

Grover Dalton eyed the ominous buildup of brooding black thunderheads on the southern horizon. "Oh, Lord, don't let them come our way," he asked fervently.

Nine fallen angels, two large wagons, a big black gelding, packhorse and a dog of half-wolf parentage made a strange caravan. Stranger still to be headed up by what appeared to be a slim-waisted young man in his late teens. A flash of auburn hair showed under the tan Stetson the trail boss wore, and the smallness of the glove-covered hands and booted feet suggested a bit of effeminacy, as did the gestures. Closer, careful scrutiny would have revealed that the traveling band consisted of ten women, without a single man to care for them or do the hard work. The teams of draft animals seemed not to mind.

They made good time, headed southeast out of Campo, Colorado. On the first day, Charity Rose pushed the caravan hard, putting all the distance possible between them and the town, which held no pleasant memories. At the last moment, Charity had nearly had a fight on her hands convincing some of the girls not to pay a last visit to Lane Everets. She hoped that distance would make the memories fainter.

"Charity, what do we eat tonight?" Tina asked plaintively from the seat of the first wagon.

"I, ah, haven't thought of it. We brought plenty of supplies. But I suppose I could ride ahead and see what I can kill."

"*Kill?* You mean kill something and *eat* it? How awful."

Astounded by this, Charity reined up and looked hard at the girl. "Tina, how do you suppose we get the food we eat? Haven't you ever watched your mother kill a chicken?"

Eyes wide, Tina put a hand to her mouth. "Oh, no. She'd never let us. If—if there was something dead along the road, she'd make us hide our eyes and not look at it."

"You poor child. Somehow you'll have to learn a lot about life. I think maybe four rabbits or a dozen quail would do us nicely. Perhaps some nice, plump doves. Is there a shotgun in that wagon?"

"Yes-um," Tina answered in a faraway tone.

"Let me have it," Charity commanded.

That night, with the wagons drawn close into a V at the steep bank of a creek, they dined on whole roasted quail, fried potatoes and onions, and honey-dipped corn bread. All the girls swore they had never had anything so elegant and delicious when Lane Everets had been around. Even Tina overcame her squeamishness enough to devour three of the tasty little birds. Evette, whose café au lait complexion and watch spring-curled hair revealed her distant African ancestry, summed it up most aptly.

"Lawdy, ladies, we've for sure never et so well before. We's better off than we ever was."

Morning found them on the road shortly after the sun rose.

Two nights following the abortive raid on Hopewell, the disgruntled citizens of Cottonwood Springs still licked their wounds. The nucleus of the county-seat movement sat around in the parlor of Otto Blutcher's home, drinking from bottles of tepid beer and offering impossible schemes for recovering what they saw as rightfully *their* records. The business of the meeting got exactly nowhere. Shortly after nine o'clock, a knock sounded at the door. Otto smoothed his thick blond hair and rose, his heavy German belly preceding him as he crossed to admit the visitor.

A stranger entered, a dapper-dressed man in a sportily cut coat and narrow-legged trousers, his brocaded vest of gray and maroon stylishly set off with a ruffled and lace-trimmed white shirt and cordovan string tie. He held a low-crowned gray felt boater in one hand and flashed a wide white smile.

"Gentlemen, I imagine you are all curious as to why I am here. Let me explain and I'm sure we shall come to a meeting of minds. I am Maurice Descoines of New Orleans, at your service. I have an interesting proposition to present to you."

"Oh? What's that?" Karl Richter asked in an argumentative tone.

"Ah, monsieur, my condolences on your, ah, injury. It was caused in the defense, the futile defense, of the county records, was it not?"

"You come here to insult us, an' you're goin' home with your asshole up around your ear lobes," Josh Harper growled.

"*Non, non, non*, my friends. I commiserate with your problems and only wish to assist in a manner I am sure will be mutually rewarding."

"What's all them fancy words mean?" Ruben Fenn asked, scratching behind his left ear.

"Let me explain," Frenchy Descoines offered grandly. "My principal, the man I represent, has taken into account the flux of county seats in the western part of the state and has decided to take a hand. His services and those of his men would not come cheaply, however. That cost could be offset by other, ah, arrangements, however. It is that matter I have come here to discuss."

"What do you mean by 'other arrangements?' " Karl Richter inquired.

"There is sure to be some means of revenue to be achieved from the final establishment of the county seat location, is there not? Well, then, a suitable reward for assisting in this resolution would not be out of order, I'm sure. Other counties have undertaken to use outside protection for their partisan support of a county seat. For instance, the town of Ingalls has retained the services of William Barclay Masterson, William Tilghman and other notable gunmen to support their claim to the Gary County seat. Their fees were not a matter of public disclosure, though I assure you it amounted to more than a hundred dollars a week per man."

"Bat Masterson, well I'll be damned," Dallas Avery blurted out.

His heavily bandaged shoulder still hurt him considerably, and he frowned in an attempt to fight back the pain. After the disaster of the ambush, Dallas was ready to accept any idea that held a promise of success. He wondered who this Descoines fellow represented and put it into a question.

"William Andrew Baudine," Descoines answered simply.

"Vould he also be known as Concho Bill Baudine?" Otto Blutcher asked shrewdly.

"Ah . . . the accolade has been applied to him, yes. Why does that disturb you so?"

"The man is an outlaw, a gunman," Blutcher sputtered.

Descoines produced the fleeting ghost of a smile. "Is Masterson, or Tilghman or any of the others much different? Yet they are presently respected lawmen and keepers of the peace. Who is to say what Mr. Baudine may be tomorrow morning? A lot could depend upon you and what you *said* he might be, eh? I suggest we look further into that aspect. Before I'm done tonight, there should be a meeting of the minds."

Chapter Nine

Billows of red-brown dust rose from the unusual caravan as it traveled eastward into the narrow panhandle of Indian territory. For two days they had seen no other humans. Charity hoped it would remain so, at least until they turned northward and entered Kansas. She was not a great trailblazer, she admitted to herself if not to the soiled doves who depended upon her. For that reason she had chosen to take the same route they had previously traveled, on a known road, rather than strike due east from Colorado to Kansas.

One good thing had come from the hurried schedule she had enforced. Travel fatigue soon reduced the amount of bickering among the fallen angels. Although they were sisters under the sheets, so to speak, the personality differences and personal quirks of the bawds created a constant, if not violent, friction. Charity had to admit that she generally found their conversation, often spiced with racy and lascivious observations, to be preferable to that of the prim and proper matrons she had encountered through most of her life. What could be more boring than discussing the advantage of using sal soda instead of baking powder, or the virtues of one type of cloth over another in making aprons? But once the natural drivers had emerged among her charges, she had the advantage of being able to ride out ahead and avoid the constant clack and clatter of their discourse.

In so doing, on their fifth day out from Campo, she was first to spot a huge cloud of dust hanging on the eastern horizon. It seemed to stretch for two miles or more, north to south, across their route. The image of a raging dust storm formed in Charity's mind. Then she considered it might be a last, pitiful herd of buffalo, locked into their endless, seasonal migration. She fervently hoped it wasn't the other alternative: a band of hostile Indians.

With that unpleasant thought uppermost, Charity reined Lucifer around and cantered back to the wagons to inform the girls of the possible danger. Most of them took it well. Tina hid herself in the rear wagon awhile and cried. Charity's promise of fresh, rich buffalo meat if it turned out to be such soon brought her forth. When they camped for the night, the dust cloud remained on the horizon, having come no nearer other than their gain on it.

At midmorning the next day Charity came upon a wide, well-beaten path, grooved deep into the prairie. Due north, ahead of it, the dust rose in the air. At once she realized the meaning behind it all and chided herself for unnecessary worry. Once again she hurried back to the wagons.

"What we have," she happily informed her flock of doves, "is a cattle drive. For as long as we can, we'll travel in their wake and the way will be clear for us. Better than an eastern turnpike."

"How's that?" Zelda, the doubter, asked.

"No tolls to pay," Charity answered cheerfully.

Through the remainder of the day the wagons rolled easily along the broad trail of the cattle. At nightfall, they angled out from behind the slow-moving herd, far enough to find forage for their animals. The wranglers' campfire could be seen as a far off pink glow on the northern horizon. It at once became the subject of excited, and speculative, talk among the freelance drabs.

"Maybe we ought to pay a call on them?" Penelope Saunders suggested. "Those boys ought to be downright horny enough to jump outta their britches."

"What if they don't have any money?" Helen Moran complained. "We ain't about to do work on credit?"

"Why do you girls have to consider that prospect at all?" Charity inquired from across the low fire where the women had gathered.

All nine returned her looks blankly. "Because," Charlie Cramer explained as though to a backward child, "that's what we do."

"Uh . . . I, ah, see," Charity responded, nonplussed. "But is it necessary? Helen might be right. Maybe they couldn't pay you for your, ah, services."

With a merry twinkle in her eyes, Amanda LaDoux, who styled herself as Evette, expressed the group's financial philosophy. "Honey, if they's got the will, we'll find a way."

Grover Dalton tossed the dregs from his coffee cup onto the ash-covered coals of the morning cook fire. "Better head 'em up, boys. That shower last night was gentle enough, only I don't like the looks of what's buildin' to the southwest. We've a ways to go, with the Kansas border still waitin' for us."

"Mister Dalton, is it true the Jayhawkers could seize our cattle and kill 'em?" young Peter Norton asked.

"They could, Petey," Dalton answered shortly. "They'd soon know as well as we do that there's no tick fever among these critters. They'd kill a few to make a show for us, then sell the rest for their own profit. That's the way it's been since the trouble first started."

"But—that's dishonest," Peter blurted in his innocence.

"What do you expect from Jayhawkers? Dirty, Yankee, abolitionist scum," Taters Gorman, the cook, growled.

Taters had served with General Hood's Texans. He'd lost one leg at the knee during the battle of Pea Ridge and stumped around on a wooden peg. Stories had it that Taters had owned a respectable spread before the War. Carpetbaggers had stolen it from him, as they had from thousands of others, during Reconstruction. He'd never forgiven the Yankees for it—in particular those who had sided with the wild-eyed fanatic John Brown. Disabled though he might be, Taters' condition hadn't affected his gun hand. The occasion of his third killing of a "Jayhawker" in Abilene had resulted in his banning from Kansas.

Enough years had passed now for Grover Dalton to feel safe in taking the grizzled old man back on this drive. The fire in his response to Peter Norton gave the trail boss cause to wonder if he'd made the right decision. At least, he consoled himself, they couldn't ask for better food than Taters dished out.

"Don't mind him, Petey," Dalton injected. "Taters has a read hard-on for those Kansas gentry. Though these days I figure he's more bark than bite."

"Am I? Am I? Well now, Mister Grover Dalton, you might just wait and see," Taters challenged.

"There'll be no huntin' down Jayhawkers, Taters. If they come after us, we'll take the fight to them. Otherwise, we leave 'em alone. Y'hear?" Dalton dictated.

His nearly toothless mouth working in agitation, Taters Gorman cast his glance toward the ground and made busy with breaking down his cooking gear. "Have it your way, by dangit. You al'ays do. Have it your way and watch what happens. They'll be down on us like stink on a skunk. You wait and see."

Within half an hour the herd had been formed up for the trail. Dalton took his accustomed place at the head of the long line of lowing, shuffling animals. Taters Gorman started off with the chuck wagon. He could make far better time than the slow-moving cattle. The men had biscuits, cold beef and dried apples to munch at their nooning, stored in small, grease-stained coffee sacks slung around their necks. Taters would set up at the new bedding ground and have supper well on the way by the time the herd reached that spot. It was the ritual of the drive, enacted every day since the large gather left Texas in early spring with frost still on the tall gama grass.

"Mo-o-ove 'em out!" Grover Dalton sang out.

With yips, whistles and bawling sounds, the drovers set the mass of hoofed gold into motion. The pall of dust instantly began to rise. They'd been lucky so far, Dalton reflected for the hundredth time. Not a man lost to sickness, rattlesnakes or stampede. At this rate, they might make it all the way. While the hours slowly advanced, Grover Dalton recalled the excitement he had felt on the drives of his youth, and before he realized it, the sun stood at its midday zenith.

Looking around, he signaled for the bellwether to be headed in and the herd stopped for a brief half hour. "Take the noon break in usual shifts, boys," he instructed the drovers.

Grover chewed reflectively on his own portion of beef and biscuit, eyes constantly roving over the brown, black and rust backs of the milling herd. The storm clouds of dawn had dissipated, raining themselves out long before arriving in their area. He hardly noticed the rattle of wheels and tramp of approaching horses from along their back trail. The surprised remarks and low whistles of his trail crew alerted him to an extraordinary event.

"Good morning," came the husky-voiced greeting from what appeared to be a slightly built young man astride a big black gelding. "So you're the dust cloud we've been seeing since yesterday."

"Howdy. We're taking our noonin', if you've a mind to step down and rest," Grover managed, still not believing what his eyes revealed in the wagons. "Be mighty quiet, though. You could spook the cattle."

"I'm C. M. Rose," the stranger offered along with an extended hand. "These, ah, young ladies are traveling with me to Kansas."

"Grover Dalton. You're a ways from your home, I gather."

"Arizona's where I hang out," Charity told him. "The girls come from, ah, everywhere."

"Ummmm. I bet they do," Grover responded, certain, if unwilling to believe, that providence had delivered a whole slew of painted ladies into their midst.

"How'd your boys like a little entertainment tonight?" Zelda asked boldly from the lead wagon.

By God, he'd been right, Grover concluded. The eager mutters among the trail crew made it obvious how they felt about the prospect. Grover had visions of a wild orgy, of a stampede and disaster. He started to defuse the situation before it became too late.

"I'm not so sure that would be a good idea. It's all rather irregular."

"A man's got to grasp what's at hand, ain't that right, Charity?" Zelda goaded.

Charity? On closer scrutiny, Grover realized that the young "man" was in fact a quite beautiful young woman. Another one. That made ten drabs to service his twenty-three-man crew. Expectant expressions on the faces of the men convinced Grover he'd have worse trouble on his hands if he chased them off entirely. Reluctantly, Grover relented a small bit.

"It wouldn't be wise for you to set up right in our camp. The noise of the, ah, festivities could easily disturb the beeves. They haven't any brains and the slightest shadow or softest sound can sometimes put them on the prod."

"No concern there," Zelda assured him. "We can set up some distance away and the boys take turns payin' us a call. We've worked it that way on times before."

"Well, ah, you seem to know what you're about, young lady," Grover acknowledged.

"You just bet we do. And I'll be expectin' you to call on me first off, big boy. See you fellas, now," Zelda taunted.

"Take your rigs about a mile north of where you'll see our chuck wagon stopped. That'll be our beddin' ground, and the distance ought to be enough to be safe," Grover instructed.

Charity nodded curtly and swung back into the saddle. Grover tipped his hat, a knowing grin splitting his face. Peter Norton came up to the trail boss, removed his hat and wiped at the sweat-soaked band.

"Miss Charity, is it? he said in a tone of love-struck youth. "At first I thought she was a boy, and that bothered me, 'cause I also thought she was real pretty."

"Want to run that one past me again, son?" Grover teased.

"I'm glad she's a she, Mister Dalton. And I think I'm fallin' in love," Peter elaborated with a mixture of misery and wonder.

"This whole thing is as harebrained as any I've ever heard of," Charity complained when they stopped for an early camp.

Most of the girls had hurried off to a nearby creek to bathe, primp and pretty up. Charity, Charlie and Zelda remained behind. The youthful jades seemed eager as bridesmaids for the evening to come. For her own part, Charity wanted nothing to do with it. Zelda and Charlie had insisted, with urging from Clarisse, Evette and Monique, that she collect and hold the money for them.

Charity had refused.

"You're not being fair," Charlie pouted. "You've taken Lane's place and it's up to you to see we don't get cheated or hurt."

"Then don't do it!" Charity had snapped back. "You know how I feel. I think that a woman selling her body is degrading. You shouldn't . . . shouldn't . . ."

"You think begging is more noble?" Nichole asked nastily, hands on hips.

"What are we supposed to *do?* We don't know anything else," wailed Adrianne.

From there the argument degenerated into a repetition of all previous ones. In the end, Charity relented. She had to admit she didn't know what else to do. Now the girls made ready while she saw to preparing supper.

Shortly after sundown the first nervous, exhilarated cowboys arrived. Zelda collected the money, three dollars each, to hold while they took their selections away to the partitioned-off cubicles in the wagons. Soon more arrived, then more, until each of the nine tarts had accepted a customer, with some waiting in line. Against her protests, Charity had to accept the booty while Zelda and a lanky Texan went off to find a convenient bush to hide behind.

"Well, uh, that sort of leaves us, er, alone," a soft, boyish voice spoke behind her.

Startled, Charity turned to see a blushing youngster, slim and sunburned, his eyes gazing down at his boot toes rather than examining her with the lust of his companions. The contrast brought a smile to Charity's lips.

"I'm Charity Rose."

"Peter. Peter Norton. The crew calls me Petey," he went on, flushing darkly. "That makes me feel like a little boy. And . . . I'm not. I, ah, I sort of, ah, didn't know how to, er, go about it, I guess. Everybody beat me to it. I mean . . ." He broke off miserably.

"I understand. You only have so much time, so the others can be relieved from the herd."

"Th-that's right. And if I . . . well, the other fellers will . . ."

"You'll have a chance for a turn," Charity tried to assure him.

"Well, ah, I don't know, er, well, ah, if I saw anyone I, ah, liked that much." The blush bloomed into full-faced scarlet.

Something stirred deep within Charity, and she stepped close to this shy youth, taken suddenly by his clean, innocent good looks. She reached out and lightly touched his cheek.

"I—I, well I . . ." Peter blurted. "That is, ah, not among those I saw."

"You mean there's someone else who's already captured your heart?" Charity teased lightly, thinking of a girl back home.

"Yes, there is. Only . . . I don't know . . . how to—to go about . . . *asking you!*" Peter wailed in utter discomfort.

For the moment, the earth might have opened and swallowed her, Charity thought. She'd hardly expected this turn. Yet her body rapidly awakened to the sensual messages radiated by his eager, youthful personality. Her nostrils flared and she caught a draught of that magic elixir that so few had ever generated for her. Memory provided delightful images.

Corey Willis. Oh, he'd had it in abundance. For as long as two full years before their first bold coupling, she had smelled that special aroma around Corey. And Tom. Dear, sweet Tom Thornton. His male muskiness had made her dizzy-headed from the first time he'd courted her, when she'd turned fifteen. Then there'd been Bob Carroll. Just the thought of him made her stomach squirm. So few men, yet so very much loving. Her heart near to burst as she reached out to draw Peter close to her breast.

"Would it be your, ah, first time?" she asked gently, almost afraid to hear the answer. Her heart had begun to pound.

"N-no. Not—not really. It'd be m-my second, you see," Peter answered wretchedly. "B-but you're so pretty, and so d-d-different from the others. I just don't *know!*"

Charity noted that no one waited outside the rear portion of the far wagon. Quickly she took Peter's hand and drew him along. "Hurry. Come with me. And . . . be quiet," she commanded.

Chapter Ten

"Come on, time's up," Charity commanded with a rap on the thick wooden side of the wagon. "Hop out of there, both of you. We've got to make ready for the new bunch."

They'd all be smirking at her tomorrow, Charity admitted irritably as she helped Peter into the rear of the wagon box. Perky little Charlie had given her an "I told you so" leer as she'd climbed out with her cowboy lover. Damn them, she didn't care what they thought. Her body had betrayed her, and she had no power over that. Her body and that of the thin, wiry youth with the deep, soulful blue eyes and soft, white-blond hair. Peter reminded her so much of Corey. Her clothes came off with swift ease, while Peter fumbled at his in uncertainty.

"Let me help," Charity suggested in a whisper.

"N-n-no. If you did, the way I feel right now, I'm afraid I'd . . . I'd, ah, you know, before we even got started."

Charity wanted to laugh. She wanted to cry. She longed to kiss him all over his skinny chest and hard, muscle-layered belly. Clear-cut lines defined the rangy strength of his arms, lard white above the wrists like his chest below his neck where his shirt protected him from the sun. Peter grunted in frustration over his belt buckle until numbed fingers remembered how to undo it. Now it was Charity's turn to experience excitement.

They kissed. The embrace went on exhaustingly until they toppled sideways onto the thick layer of goose-down comforters. Understanding Peter's inexperience and insecurity, Charity raised one leg and slowly slid the silken inner side of her thigh along the smooth outer part of his.

Peter shivered and moaned with unbridled passion as Charity used a free hand to guide him. Tears of joy formed behind his tightly closed lids and slid from the corners of Peter's eyes as he pressed forward and ever so slowly entered her.

Sweetness filled Charity's breast as she watched him. His face devoid of the harsh lines of lust, Peter held an expression of childlike innocence and bliss. As she joined her rhythm to his, he puckered his lips and closed them over one rigid nipple, making tiny, little-boy sounds of delight. For a wondrously long time, the world held still for them.

Even the harsh demands of his fast approaching climax failed to rob Peter's features of that special, angelic expression. When the savage beat of nature's drum drove them over the pinnacle, Peter still refrained from hoarse caws and earthy grunts. Gentle as a baby's breath, his words caressed Charity's ear.

"Ooh . . . oooh . . . i-it's so-o-o-o- . . . *wonderful.*"

"You're the one that's wonderful," Charity told him after reason and real time returned. "I—I want to keep you here all night, Peter."

Peter glanced down at his nakedness, suddenly embarrassed. "And I want to stay. But I'd better get back to the herd."

"How old are you, Peter? How old, really?" she inquired.

"I, er, ah, well . . . your age, I suppose."

Charity patted him on the cheek. "We'll let it go at that for now. You're right, though. You'd better dress."

"Ah, Charity, I so want to stay. There won't . . . won't be any, ah, others?"

Charity's kiss behind his ear tingled like an electric charge. "How could you think there would be? I'm not one of the girls and you're something—something special," Charity told him truthfully. "It could only happen that way. Now, good-bye. You've been so good to me."

Although the drovers and the drabs would have preferred it otherwise, the two groups of journeyers parted company early the next morning. The lightly loaded wagons could move three times faster than the cattle. Languishing sighs filled the air around the wheeled bordello the first day out. Several of the women had found cowboys they considered "sweet" or "cute" or "delightful." All agreed the Texans had conducted themselves a great deal differently than when in town at a saloon. They'd not mind repeating the performance, each admitted. It left Charity stymied. Night camp went uneventfully, neither as lively nor as profitable as the previous one, and the journeying jades started off at the crack of dawn.

Shortly after midday, Charity and her charges entered Kansas at a spot some ten miles east of Liberal. They turned northeast from there to follow Cherokee Creek. When they came upon the main road to Ford County, they'd take it north to Dodge City. Although the terrain remained much like that they had traveled through in Indian Territory, new and disturbingly unusual sights stirred their attention.

"Oh, look!" Tina called from the lead wagon. "Look at them. All white and still. What are they?"

"Buffalo bones," Charity informed her, recalling stories she had read in issues of *The Gentlemen Farmer, Harpers* and other New York magazines. "The hiders have been here, hunting the great herds."

Scraps of yellowed sinew and dessicated flesh showed in places among the myriad rib cages and huge pelvic bones. Stretched endlessly along their route, the skeletal monuments to the great bison swarm that had once blackened the prairie created a grim forest.

"It—it's so sad," Tina replied after a long moment of thought.

"Yes. Except for the contract hunters who provided for railroad crews, they didn't take the meat. Left it to rot," Charity answered coldly.

All they had wanted were the hides. Belts made of buffalo hide were in big demand to turn the wheels of industry. Civilization depended upon them, said such men as John J. Astor III and other American entrepreneurs. Rarely did anyone mention the primary reason behind the extermination of the buffalo, Charity considered with some rancor.

Disposing of the bison deprived the Plains Indians of their source of food, lodging, implements, some weapons and many religious articles. It left them starving, impoverished and totally dependent on the white man for handouts. And it made it easy to break treaties and open more land for westward expansion. Charity had had enough experience with the Apaches not to be overly swayed by stories of the plight of the "noble redman." Yet her innate sense of right and justice rebelled at such a callous means of disposing of a whole people who stood in the way of the ambitions of an avaricious few.

"How far do we have to go to get away from these

awful things?" Zelda's question, tinged with repugnance, interrupted Charity's reflections.

"I don't know. I read an article once that said the bones went on for miles. The writer told how they traveled for two days without an end to them," Charity informed her.

"Can't we find another road?"

"I'm sure we can, Zelda. But it will make it difficult to get to Dodge City," Charity answered. "Cheer up, they're only bones."

Hypocrite, she chided herself at this flip observance.

"Ugh. I know *that*. What I want is to get away from them."

"Think about something else, Zelda," Charity suggested brightly.

"Yeah. Like the *fun* you had last night?" Zelda came back.

Evette giggled. "A girl can't get nowhere *givin'* it away, honey."

"I ought to pop you in the mouth for that," Charity said, aggravated. "If I wasn't trying to show you that you can have a better way of life, I would, too." A waterfall of tittering answered her. "All right. I lost control. I found myself with someone who . . . who reminded me of, ah, someone, and—and the next thing I knew, I couldn't help myself. That's all there is to it."

"Who's that *someone,* Charity?" Nichole asked.

"Tell us, Charity," Charlie urged. "Tell it all."

"I will . . . sometime," Charity responded, smiling for the first time in a while.

They made night camp on a low, tree-shaded bluff that overlooked a quiet, sandy-bottomed eddy in Cherokee Creek. After the usual chores, Charity led four of the girls down to a welcome bath. They sudsed and splashed in the cool, shallow water and talked lightly of their lives before joining up with Lane Everets' traveling brothel.

Charlie, whose delightful curves moved gracefully through the liquid medium, came at last to Charity's side.

"Now, Charity. You must tell us all about that special someone," she pleaded.

"Well . . . I don't know," Charity began.

Her eyes took on a faraway look, and a gentle smile creased her lips. Pale white hair floated around Corey Willis' perfectly shaped head as he galloped over the desert. Already he had removed his shirt, and his browned body glistened in the sunlight. Gradually the images became more distinct as Charity told of her first, overpowering love.

"His name was Corey. We were thirteen," she informed the bevy of tarts. "It wasn't exactly that we were in love. We were young and healthy and . . . curious. Our bodies . . . demanded what our minds didn't yet understand. Even the touch of Corey's hand on my arm sent shivers through me. One day we started daring each other to go skinny-dipping together at our swimming hole. One thing led to another, and when we touched our bare bodies from shoulders to toes, I thought I'd go mad from the thrill. It didn't take long after that before we . . . And afterward, we talked. After that we . . . we could never get enough of each other."

For long minutes Charity cast her spell over her audience. They listened avidly to each little detail. When at last she came to her bittersweet parting from Corey, not a one of the hardened working girls lacked tears in her eyes. A protracted silence hung on the evening air, water gurgling around their sylphlike bodies while the sky turned magenta, umber and purple. At last, Charlie Cramer put a hand on Charity's cheek.

"Oh, that's so sad, Charity. Beautiful, but sad," she sighed.

"You could write a book about that," Clarisse suggested. "One of those bedside romances."

Tina giggled. "Yeah. With all the steamy details."

"Oh, yeah," Evette responded, with a snort of amusement. "An' every boy-kid from eleven to fifteen would be readin' it late at night under the covers and chokin' his chicken till he rubbed it raw."

"Enough!" Charity exclaimed as she rose and sought out a towel. "We'd better be getting back. I'm sure the rest want a bath, and there's supper to fix."

When the refreshed young ladies gained the top of the bluff, they discovered seven strange horses in camp and no sign of their sisters in sin. "Looks like our friends found something interesting to do," Evette observed, hands on her curvaceous hips.

"Entertaining customers while we lose out on the profit," Tina complained.

"That's right, ladies," a deep masculine voice declared as a tall, burly man walked from behind one wagon, adjusting his trousers. "Sheriff John Belton, at your service. My posse and I stopped off for a while to, ah, refresh ourselves."

Outmaneuvered again, Charity cast her eyes heavenward in supplication.

"Sit down, Mister Baudine," Karl Richter boomed pleasantly. "You'll pardon my clumsiness with this damned shot-up arm. Help yourself. There's bourbon, pear brandy, and homemade beer."

"Thank you," Concho Bill responded. "Bourbon will be right fine. You have a nice home here, Mister Richter."

"I appreciate that, Mr. Baudine. In particular from a man of taste like your representative, Descoines, and yourself. Well now, I'll have me a tot of that pear brandy if you'll pour, and we can get down to business."

"A man after my own heart," Concho Bill allowed. He poured three stiff fingers into a water glass and shoved it over the polished rosewood table to his host.

"Mister Descoines mentioned that compensation for your men would be high. He also said there were ways to offset some of that. I'm interested in what you have in mind."

A wolfish grin spread over Baudine's handsome face. He leaned forward and the lamplight shimmered off the iridescent color of his silk, waist-length jacket. His cold gray eyes glittered with barely suppressed avarice.

"One of the hazards to gentlemen in our calling is an unsympathetic attitude on the part of lawmen. Whenever it's possible, we like to establish a climate of understanding and friendly accord with the local officers of the law. That allows us to indulge in other means of making a profit with, ah, shall we say, impunity."

Richter's big ham hand engulfed his glass, and he took a long draw on the contents before speaking. "You're saying that you want the law to look the other way if you knock over a stage or clean out a bank? Is that it?"

Baudine's full, sensual lips formed a moue of distaste. "Crudely put, but accurate."

"Certainly that wouldn't include those facilities serving our community?"

"Oh, definitely not. The Chinese have a proverb that says a wise bird never shits in its own nest."

Richter gave a sharp bark of laughter. "I suppose that comes from that soup they're famous for. The point is well made, though. How would you go about this, ah, supplementing your income?"

"It could be done in conjunction with your desire to obtain the county seat. What better distraction for your removal of the records than a bank robbery?"

"By damn, I like that," Richter enthused. "Would that

be the only instance?"

"Not at all," Baudine assured him. "We could take our pick of suitable places and always have a safe home to return to for as long as we were needed to insure your claim to the county seat."

Richter rubbed his hands together enthusiastically. "You know, I think we're going to do business together quite well."

A shout of alarm from outside interrupted Concho Bill's reply. There followed the thump and bang of boots on the porch, and the door flew open. Buell Nolan, one of Baudine's men, entered with a youth of fourteen or so held by the scruff of the neck.

"This your brat?" he asked of Karl Richter.

"No," Richter responded. He bent forward to examine the pale-faced, frightened youth. "He ain't even from around these parts. I've seen him over in Hopewell, though."

"Yeah," the youngster summoned in defiance. "And I'm gonna tell them all about your plans, too. You can't get away with something like that."

"Is your barn occupied?" Concho Bill inquired, rising.

"Only by hay and pigs right now," Karl replied.

"Let's take this brat out there, Nolan."

"Sure, boss."

Karl Richter followed along silently, though with growing nervousness. If the Hopewell faction found out what had been discussed this night, if a lot of folks in Cottonwood Springs knew, he'd be in deep trouble. He wondered, though, what this hard man with the manners of a gentleman proposed to do about it. Inside the barn, he quickly found out.

"Put him over there," Baudine commanded.

Buell Nolan shoved the thick-shouldered youth over against a stall partition. Before the lad could raise a hand or speak in protest, Concho Bill Baudine drew his six-gun and shot the boy between the eyes.

"Bury him," the gang leader ordered. Then he placed a friendly arm around Karl Richter's shoulder and steered him toward the door. "Now, let's get back to business."

All at once, Karl Richter wanted to be sick. My God, his jumbled mind clamored, what had he gotten them into?

Chapter Eleven

Startled from his browsing by the appearance of so many humans, a small brown rabbit exploded from his nibbling pose into churning legs and laid-back ears as he dashed for safety in a wild blackberry vine. Following the commercial encounter with the posse, Charity and the doves lingered a day at their restful pool. They had located the thicket of blackberry vines, plentiful with fruit not yet ripe. The place was a delightful contrast to the miles of bleached bones. In her sleep, Charity had seen buffalo rib cages, like skeletal hands, reaching for the sky. She had awakened depressed and suggested they stay. By midafternoon they had all enjoyed the refreshing water of the creek and set about making ready to depart.

"Oh, look," Charlie called out. "There's a rider coming. He's going like blazes."

Charity glanced up to see a vaguely familiar, slight-framed person atop a galloping horse. Bits of turf flew behind the pounding hoofs. As he drew nearer, Charity recognized him as her youthful lover from the cattle drive: Peter, coming here and in quite a hurry. He reined in and dismounted before his horse came to a full stop, shouting happily to the girls. Then he saw Charity and came to her, taking both her hands in his.

"Mister Dalton sent me to find you. He begs you girls to await the arrival of our herd. Seems the boys have took to moonin' so much since you left it softened his heart and he asks if we might have one night more of pleasure in your company."

"Why, how gallant, Mister Nolan," Charity responded.

Inside, her heart pounded and she had none of the poise her cultured remark would indicate. Her loins began to tingle in anticipation of his shy yet manly loving. Peter blushed at her cool sophistication.

"Y-you will stay, then? We—we'd all be powerful obliged." Peter's boyish eagerness, his eyes fixed on her face, reflecting a compelling love, melted all hardness and resolve from Charity's heart.

"Oh, yes," she breathed out softly. "You can be sure of that."

Deputy U.S. Marshal Randolph Carter sat on a faded, tapestry-upholstered chair that smelled of dust. Opposite him, a graying woman with drawn, pinched features covered her face with her hands and sobbed wretchedly. Her thin shoulders heaved under a flour-sack print dress. Outside, on the narrow porch, several residents of Hopewell waited for the lawman's decision.

"I know something's happened to him, Marshal," the woman said in a thin voice. "Ain't like Jamie to go off and not leave word."

"When did you last see him, Miz Miller?" Marshal Carter inquired.

"Fi-five days ago," Karen Miller replied.

"Any idea when he left town?"

"No, Marshal. I, ah, there's the other children to care for. Jamie's the oldest. He sort of tends for himself."

"What about friends? Who's he run with?"

Karen Miller considered a moment. "There's Tommy Nethers, Billy Jenson, and I suppose little Danny Cook, though he's a couple of years younger than the others."

"That's a start," the marshal acknowledged. "Do you have a likeness of the boy?"

"N-no. Couldn't never afford a photo-grapher's fees," the distraught mother stated.

"Would you describe him for me?" the lawman asked.

"Well, ah, he's a bit small for his age, he's fourteen. He has light brown hair, nearly yellow, blue eyes and freckles. Small nose. He's thick chested and don't like shoes much. There's a brown-black mole, size of a ten-cent piece, over his left shoulder blade."

"Any other scars, marks, disfigurements?" the marshal inquired.

"Uh, well, ah, yes." Karen Miller blushed furiously. "The, ah, doctor, ah, insisted we have Jamie circumcised. Doctor Barnes said, uh, that, well, his, ah, machinery was too big at the front and would have caused Jamie considerable pain when he was growin' up otherwise."

Uncomfortable with such an intimate subject between a man and woman, strangers at that, Marshal Carter glanced away. "I, ah, see. Well, then, as best you know, would Jamie have been afoot?"

"No. He took that stunted little Indian pony he's had since his eleventh birthday." Again Karen Miller resorted to tears.

"Ummm. I, ah, think I have everything I need to get started, Miz Miller. Thank you for your time," Marshal Carter stated, rising. "I sympathize with your worry. It may take a day or two, but I'm positive I'll get a line on him. Good-bye, now."

Outside, the expectant townsfolk, who had summoned the marshal when Karen's concern for her missing son created a certain unease in the community, looked to the lawmen for enlightenment. He shook his head and ran a hand of blunt, thick fingers through his salt-and-pepper hair.

"Could be he's just run off," Randolph Carter opined. "Wouldn't be too unusual in a case like this. Oldest of eleven children, father gone off to escape his responsibilities. Lot of pressure on a young boy."

"I, ah," a nervous, mousy-looking man of middle age spoke up. "I didn't say anything to Karen, Marshal, but I saw Jamie ride out of town, headed over Cottonwood Springs way."

"You did?" the lawman snapped. "Did anyone try looking around over there first, before summoning me from Dodge?"

"N-no, sir. We didn't figure it was any of our business. Not until Karen started suggesting foul play," the clerkish man defended.

"Thanks, *so much*, for the help," Marshal Carter responded sarcastically. "All this time lost, when you might have found the lad." He sighed resignedly. "I'll start checking around over that way, see what develops."

Ten minutes later Marshal Carter trotted out of Hopewell, headed for Cottonwood Springs. Morning sunlight slanted over the gently undulating Kansas plains. Hawks, kites, crows and quarrelsome jays frolicked in the clear, warm air. Relaxed, Randolph Carter rode along musing over the information he had received.

Damn little, when one got down to it, he admitted. A boy, somewhat small for his age, a pony to ride, but nowhere in particular to go. He'd be used to giving orders, managing the younger children, and having more expected of him than a child could perform. If this preliminary search didn't develop any leads, he'd go back, Carter decided, and talk with Jamie's friends.

"Howdy," Marshal Carter called in greeting. Two men had ridden down a long swale and across a field of tall grass to the roadside.

"Mornin'," one squint-eyed young man returned.

"You boys from around here?" the marshal inquired.

"Yup," the second rider answered.

"Do you know the Miller boy from over Hopewell? Jamie Miller?"

"Uh ... no," the first roughly dressed fellow responded. "He in some kind of, ah, trouble, Marshal?"

Randolph Carter recalled that he had left his badge pinned to his vest front. An observant fellow like this might be useful. "No trouble. Seems he's taken off from home." He made a careful description.

"We've not seen anyone like that," came the reply. "Surely not in the last day or two. We're ridin' line on Mr. Hardesty's place."

"Jamie's been gone for five days now. Think back," Carter urged.

Frowns of concentration wrinkled the ranch hands' brows. Each shook his head in the negative. "Sounds familiar," the older of the pair declared. "Might of come across him at another time."

"Sorry we couldn't be of more help, Marshal," the younger added.

"Obliged anyhow, boys. I'll be gettin' along."

Marshal Carter gained little from his preliminary investigation. No one, it seemed, had seen or heard of little Jamie Miller. The third day of the marshal's activities brought him to the edge of Cottonwood Springs. At a farm on the fringe of town—the residence within the city limit, the fields spread beyond—he managed to casually observe the livestock in a corral some distance from the main buildings. Among the draft horses and buggy teams he noticed a short-legged, piebald, shaggy mustang. The animal showed the whites of its eyes when he called to it using the name Mrs. Miller had provided him. Deep in thought, Marshal Carter departed at once for Hopewell.

There he gathered Jamie's friends, Tommy Nethers and Danny Cook. Quickly he outlined the situation. Both boys reacted with surprise and signs of worry. Tommy licked his lips with a pink wedge of tongue and spoke, the freckles on the bridge of his pug nose wriggling.

"No, sir. We don't have any idea of where Jamie might be. At least *I* don't. I hadn't seen him for a few days, then Miz Miller came askin' about him. Is he hurt or something?"

"We're not sure, Tommy. How about you, Danny?" the lawman asked.

The smaller lad ran short, fat fingers through a thatch of long, straight, coppery hair, the severely bitten nails snagging here and there. He wrinkled up his face and produced a winsome smile that revealed large, rounded front teeth. His stocky build and better than average clothing gave him the look of a miniature adult male rather than a little boy.

"Last I saw Jamie was Saturday a week ago. We went skinny-dipping in the crick."

"How long did you stay there?"

"Oh, from right around eleven until late in the afternoon. Too long, anyway, 'cause I got my butt sunburned."

Tommy broke up in shrill guffaws, and the marshal waited before posing his next question.

"The last time either of you saw Jamie, did he seem unhappy about anything? Was he down in the mouth over something that happened at home or in school?"

"N-no-oo," both youngsters drawled out.

"You don't sound so sure," Carter prompted.

"Well, ah," Danny began hestitantly, a blush blooming on both round cheeks. "His sister, Daphne, caught him chokin' his chicken in the haymow. But he told me he made her promise not to tell or he'd let their mother know that it was Daphne who knocked over the crock of cottage cheese, not raccoons who got into it in the springhouse." He paused a moment, brow creased, then brightened, eyes shining. "If she told anyway, he might have been afraid of the strap or something."

Marshal Carter considered that a moment. Danny certainly had the details of that incident. Had Jamie confided something else to him because of it? "That sounds mighty thin a reason for running away from home," he suggested.

"Not to me," Danny came back. "*I* got walloped good when Maw caught me doin' it. If something like that happened again, I'd want to get away."

"Me, too," Tommy agreed. "My Paw sure whales the tar outta me with his razor strop when I do somethin' wrong."

Boys saw things from a different perspective than adults, Carter allowed. He changed the subject. "Can one of you describe Jamie's pony for me?"

"Sure," they answered together.

Tommy swiftly sketched a description that matched the pony Marshal Carter had seen at the farm outside Cottonwood Springs. That did not bode well, but he tried not to show his reaction. He thanked the boys and hurried to the livery stable.

Twilight settled over the West Kansas prairie by the time U.S. Marshal Carter arrived at the farm that had piqued his curiosity. He waited until full darkness before he rode in close. When no lights appeared in the house, he moved in with confidence. He tied his horse behind the barn, considering it the most unlikely avenue of approach. Then he checked the horses in the corral.

One of the buggy teams was gone. The pony remained, along with plow horses and a mare that appeared to be close to foaling. Sticking to the shadows, he walked to the barn and entered through a small side door.

Marshal Carter didn't know exactly what he searched for. Any indication, however small, that might point to the whereabouts of the boy would satisfy him. He lighted a lantern, which he shielded with his corduroy coat, and began to look around. When he encountered the irregular, mounded earth in the rear stall, a chill slid along his spine. Hoping to be mistaken, he located a shovel and began to uncover the loose soil.

Sweat stained the armpits of his shirt and dripped from his face when Marshal Carter snagged the shovel edge on a button. Reluctantly, he dropped to his knees and brushed with his hands to reveal the dead features of Jamie Miller. The boy's skull was oddly distorted, having been shot between the eyes. He opened the corpse's trousers to verify the identification. No accident this, the marshal acknowledged.

Who would murder a small boy? And why? The questions haunted Randolph Carter as he covered the corpse. Once he completed the grisly task, he made efforts to remove any sign of his presence. He'd find out who occupied the farm and come back with warrants for their arrest. He hung the lantern on a nail and lowered the wick. He was leaning up to blow out the flame when the door creaked open.

"Hold it right there," K. C. Honeywell snarled from the doorway.

"I'm a United States Marshal," Randolph Carter replied calmly. "Put up your gun."

"Not likely," Honeywell sneered as he squeezed the trigger of his .45 Colt.

Two hundred fifty-five grains of lead spat from the muzzle and struck U.S. Marshal Carter in the side of his head. His skull bulged and blood sprayed from his nose, mouth and ears. A flap of skin and bone popped from the opposite side and sprayed the barn wall with brain tissue and rose-tinted fluid. For a long moment, the dead peace officer remained standing; then he crumpled and dropped in a heap, his life fluid staining the straw.

Despite Concho Bill Baudine's orders, word of the killing quickly spread to Cottonwood Springs. Karl Richter, Otto Blutcher and a committee of six men representing the county-seat adherents came to the Baudine's hangout, angry and upset over the cold-blooded murder of a United States Marshal. Baudine met them with an icy glower.

"Have you taken leave of your senses?" Richter demanded. "That man was a federal officer. We'll have everyone, including the army, down around our necks if this gets out."

"He was prowling in *your* barn," Baudine answered calmly. "And you know what could come of that. My man had no choice."

"It's all over town now. Consider our futures, our lives, if the government ever learns about it," Otto complained.

Baudine gave a snort of derision. "What about ours? We'd be the ones to hang."

"Ve, ah . . . vell, that is, ah . . ." Blutcher stammered.

Thinking fast, a plan bloomed, half-formed, in Baudine's mind. "You two disgust me. You come here whining about the risk. *There is no risk* . . . not to you. One thing, we have to make sure nothing about this gets out of town. Richter, I want you, and your fine committee here, to see to it no one leaves who would carry any tales about a U.S. Marshal, and any mail that goes out is read first."

"Bu-but, that's against the law," Richter protested.

"You go ahead and do it, there might be some new law in Cottonwood Springs before long," Baudine returned ominously.

Still discontent, muttering to themselves, the citizens'

committee members allowed themselves to be ushered out of the farmhouse. Once they departed, Concho Bill called a council of war.

"Boys, these weak-sister farmers and soft-handed townies will lose their nerve in a day or so. What they need is a little backbone to enforce the regulations the way we want them to be. Looks like we might wind up with a town of our own. Get everyone ready and we'll go see what we can do about that."

Chapter Twelve

Whippoorwills, loons and owls vied with each other to bring haunting music to the star-speckled night. Near the camp, cattle lowed in contentment, resting from the day of constant walking. Eager cowboys huddled around the cook fire, sipping coffee and waiting their turn to visit the distant encampment where for the third time in the past week the joys of the flesh awaited them. The Kansas prairie hummed and clicked with the sound of insects. Grover Dalton hunkered down with his men. His mustaches drooped low beside his mouth, and he wiped at them after taking a long draw on his coffee.

Of late, his own natural urges had been getting to him. He longed for the warm, soft comfort of a woman, yet doggedly maintained his faithfulness to his wife, Lavinia. How far away Texas seemed, when the rich perfume of lusty, willing ladies wafted to him on the evening breeze. Lucky kid, that Petey Norton. He'd managed to strike sparks off the only one of those women not a working girl. No sharing for him. As a reward for his second, harrowing high-speed ride to reach the bevy of doves and have them remain, Dalton had given Peter the entire night to pursue his desires. Yep, a lucky kid.

Over at the traveling-bordello encampment, Peter Norton had only begun to discover how deep his good fortune ran. He sat, entranced, in the rear portion of a large wagon. He wore only his white cotton long-john bottoms and long, red-top socks, which he was in the process of removing. The front of his woolen underdrawers towered upward like a bedouin's tent. From beyond the hanging blanket partition came the sounds of rough and hurried passion. Across from him, gleaming golden in the lamplight, the naked form of Charity Rose glowed with an amber nimbus, much like Peter as a boy had imagined angels to appear. His hands trembled with the urgency of his actions.

"Here, let me help you," Charity offered, placing a soft, warm hand on his wrist.

Peter sighed contentedly and leaned back while Charity removed his stockings. "I still can't believe it. Getting the whole night."

"You deserve it," Charity told him. "To ride so hard twice in a row only two days apart isn't an easy thing." Then she slid questing fingers below the elastic band at the top of his underwear.

Slowly she pulled the long johns downward, revealing his rigid maleness pulsing with the power of infatuation-fueled lust. When she had him completely bare, Charity came closer, hovering over his supine form between his upraised knees. As though in a dream, she languidly bent forward.

Wet and cool at first, her lips shocked him as they covered the sensitive flesh of his engorged knob. Peter began to writhe in growing ecstasy. He'd never had such a thing done to him and he felt his heart would burst. With no mind to hurry, Charity slowly pleasured her young lover. Peter moaned, then thrust lightly with his hips.

Worms of pleasure crawled upward through his belly, expanding into his chest.

Charity shivered in her own delight as her tongue worked its magic on Peter's flesh with an almost imperceptible motion. Seconds became minutes, which slid by in a steamy euphoria. Peter cried out in heightened response and clasped both hands behind Charity's head. He began to pump his hips, driving his fevered penis deep within while she worked with increasing fervor to draw him to an explosive completion.

Frenzied, in a maelstrom of mutual delight, the happy lovers toiled in the fields of Eros until the magic moment when the world lurched sideways for Peter and his body heaved in mighty convulsions of release. He shuddered and whimpered and eased down the incline to calm bemusement. A strong gust of cold wind rocked the wagon, and in the distance thunder rumbled broodingly. When reality returned, Peter found Charity lying full length at his side.

"I've never . . . er, that is, the f-first time I've had that happen," Peter whispered softly. "It was like nothing else in the world. So good, so gentle and—and *loving*."

"We've all night, Peter," Charity told him quietly. "That was only a beginning."

Midnight came to Cottonwood Springs with the desultory hooting of a single owl. Dark figures flitted through the shadows toward several houses and the doorways of all the saloons in town. In the lead, Concho Bill Baudine reached the home of Karl Richter and entered with two of his henchmen. They groped their way to the ground-floor bedroom and flung open the door. In a rush they filled the space around the bed and a lucifer match scratched to life to light a lamp. Hair tousled, Karl Richter sat upright, his face in an expression of confusion and fright. He stared alternately at the muzzles of three six-guns.

"Wh-what are you men doing here?" Richter demanded fuzzily.

"We've come to make sure there's no accidental discovery of the marshal's death. To do so," Concho Bill went on to explain, "we're taking over."

"Taking what?" Richter asked in a muddled state.

"Who are these men, Karl?" his wife asked sleepily.

"Be quiet, dear," Karl urged. "These are some of the men come to help us on the county-seat fight. Now tell me, what do you mean by 'taking over'?"

"Everything, Richter. The saloons, the bank, the stores, even the undertaking parlor. This is our town now," the outlaw informed him. "No one in, no one out, like I told you before."

"Yu-you're taking *our town?*" Richter choked out.

"Now you understand. Get your clothes on and come along. We've got a lot to do before daylight," Concho Bill commanded.

Grumbling and discontented, the group of Richter's backers, who styled themselves the county commissioners, gathered along with the mayor, city council and town marshal in the Persian Palace saloon, under smoky kerosene lamps. Angry voices buzzed and raised in pitch to a rumble; then a few shouts blared above the general noise. This continued until Concho Bill climbed atop the bar and K. C. Honeywell fired a shot into the ceiling.

"Hear, O Israel, hear the word of the Lord!" K. C. intoned quite inaccurately.

"All of you shut up and listen. From here on, your lives depend on what I'm going to say," Concho Bill yelled. When the room quieted, he went on. "From here on, me and my boys are in charge of this town. Nobody leaves and any strangers who come here stay. Yesterday evening,

Mister Richter and Blutcher tried to break the contract the city has with us. The only way we can see that it is carried out is to take control of the community. Everything will be as it was, except for a few minor changes."

"Such as what?" Ambrose Slocum, the mayor, demanded.

"We'll be watching the roads and patrolling the countryside around town to see no one leaves. We're going to send for a few trustworthy friends to assist us. There'll also be a check on the mail, to make sure no do-gooder takes it in mind to complain to outsiders."

"You mean about the murders?" Slocum snapped.

Concho Bill's eyes narrowed. "Mister Slocum, you're talkin' like a man who don't value life any too much. As of now, there are certain subjects that are no longer considered fit topics of conversation in Cottonwood Springs. *That's* one of them. Now then, to move along. In a few minutes, all of you, in groups of three, accompanied by my men, will go home. There you will surrender any and all firearms in your possession. Come morning the same procedure will be carried out for everyone in town. Henceforth, until such time as our contract is completed, you will consider me and my men as the law here . . . both the makers and enforcers.

"Shortly, within a few days, we will make up a force sufficient to go to Hopewell to successfully seize and hold the county records for a long enough time for the State Supreme Court to rule in your favor. Once that has been accomplished, and a sufficient profit made by us, we will depart and life can go on as before."

"Karl, what do you say about this?" Ruben Fenn demanded.

"I, er, well, Ruben, we did make an agreement to let them handle it. Maybe this is the only way to get what we want," Richter answered weakly.

"And you, Otto," Mayor Slocum prodded, "how do you feel?"

The fat German farmer shrugged thick, sloping shoulders. "It is as Karl says, *nein?* Ve asked them here and it looks now like ve haven't any choice but to try this vay and see."

"Have you lost your guts?" the angry mayor bellowed. "We're being made into captives and slaves. This man wants to turn Cottonwood Springs into an outlaw town. There are more of us than them," Slocum appealed. "We've got to stand up to them."

"Have you lost your mind?" Richter yelled back. "We haven't any way to . . ." Richter's voice cut off when Lloyd Mills, the marshal, grabbed the front of his nightshirt, stuffed hastily into a pair of trousers, and threw him into the arms of several onlookers.

"The mayor's right," Mills shouted. "We can take them!" He drew as he spoke, a fraction of a second before Dan Meeker, one of Baudine's men, put a bullet into the marshal's open mouth and blew out the back of his head.

Before most recovered from the moment of paralysis caused by the gunshot, Lloyd Mills' deputies went for their weapons. Owen Percey cut down one of them, the lawman's six-gun still in the holster. K. C. Honeywell took one ear and a large hunk of skull off the head of another. Several shots blazed then and one of the lanterns shattered, showering flaming kerosene over the man below it.

They yelled and slapped at the flames in a generally successful effort to save themselves. The third deputy died with a thin knife in his throat, thrown by Frenchy Descoines. Frightened residents of Cottonwood Springs milled about and sought some means of escape. They found Hal Newhouse barring the batwings with a sawed-off shotgun. He hefted it menacingly and discharged one barrel into the chest of a city councilman. The panicked citizens shrank back from such fearful violence. Over the pandemonium, Concho Bill shouted for order.

Mayor Slocum bent low and scooped up the marshal's handgun. He loosed a wild shot at Concho Bill, who blinked, drew with blurred speed and put a bullet through the mayor's right lung. Slocum stood a moment, staring in blank horror, before he dropped the smoking Remington .44 and reaction took over in the form of a wild leap that delivered him atop a green baize poker table. That final discharge brought silence.

"Now that we understand each other," Concho Bill said drolly, "let's get on with rounding up the firearms. Hal, I want you, Owen, Tiny Jim Boyle and Frank Drake to split up places and ride to Dodge, go down in the Nations, and go to the Missouri Brakes. Put the word out on the owlhoot that Cottonwood Springs is a place a longrider can belly up to the bar and spend a while, free from any lawman's perusal. We've got a real safe town here for them. Long as they abide by my rules, they'll be welcome."

Throughout the day, tall anvils of black-bottomed thunderheads had built in the southwest. By late afternoon they filled the entire horizon. Over at the bedding ground, Grover Dalton had doubled the night guard and limited the men's visits to the dutiful doxies to twenty minutes. All of this remained far from Peter's mind, and Charity's, as they worked feverishly with tongues and lips to give yet greater jolts of ecstasy for each one received. The world turned blinding white around them, and the air sizzled and cracked in the cacophony of a tremendous eruption of thunder close at hand. Their nostrils tingled with the scent of ozone.

"My God," Peter gasped, his voice hoarse with passion. "Did we cause that?"

Charity pushed him momentarily away and the laughter bubbled up. "No, it's only a thunderclap. Come on now, how do you want to make love?"

"We—we were doin' sort of fine the way we were, don't you think?"

"Oh, I do, I really do."

"But then, I sort of thought . . . I'd kinda like to try . . . like this," Peter suggested as he rolled onto his back and revealed his proudly upthrust member. "C'mon, straddle me and let's see how it works."

Eagerly Charity complied. This would be the greatest night of them all.

On a knoll that separated the soiled doves' camp from the bedding ground a mile away, the remains of a cottonwood tree flamed wildly after a cataclysmic lightning bolt shattered its upper branches and turned the rest into a torch. Behind it came the hissing, slashing sound of a tremendous downpour. Grover Dalton came up from his relaxed position by the fretfully whipping fire, his coffee cup still in one hand, and raised his other hand to his mouth.

Lowing and bellowing frightfully, the cattle sounded their own alarm before he could call for more men. At first a few came to their feet or bolted from a resting stance. Others soon joined in, and hoofs began to pound the ground, quickly growing louder than the approaching storm. Bawling in fear, most of the nine thousand head became a mindless mass, racing pell-mell over the rolling prairie to the north, away from the cruelty of nature.

"Stampede!" Grover Dalton yelled. "Everyone turn out.

All hands get your night horses."

A growing sickness clawed at his guts as he thought of the ten missing hands and the women who now lay helpless in the path of the crazed beasts. Another prodigious flash of white light and punishing blast drove the last of the horses and cattle into a frenzy of terror, and the world seemed to dissolve around the trail boss as he swung into his saddle.

"Oh, Christ, save us all," Dalton choked out, and it was less of an oath than a prayer.

Chapter Thirteen

Like a mighty tidal wave, great sheets of rain followed the celestial cataclysm. Wall-eyed, mindless with terror, driven ahead of the fury of the tempest, the sharp-hoofed bovines rumbled off in a northeast direction. In only seconds Grover Dalton reminded himself that the roving bordello lay directly in the path of the fear-driven cattle.

A keen sense of sickness gripped him as he realized that nothing could be done to drive the beasts away. Lurching over the ground, their panic too fresh to turn with a few shots at this point, they would be in among the wagons before any help could be organized or sent. For a moment he closed his eyes in anguish, then started to rally his men and send them after the fleeing herd.

While Dalton strove to contain the outbreak, the first few shaggy brown beasts darted erratically into the camp made by Charity and the girls. They lowed in fear and thrashed about with sharp horns. Their movements were strobe-lit into unreality by slithering bolts of lightning. Horses whinnied on the picket line and surged against restraint, sensing the deadly promise of the uncontrolled livestock. Snug in their wagon cubicle, Charity and Peter heard the horrified screams of the other girls.

"What is it?" Charity asked drowsily, her body still warm with sated passion.

"I—I'm not sure. But I think it's . . . it's a stampede. If someone doesn't turn them, these wagons won't last a minute. They'll kill us all," Peter answered, face pale, eyes gone wide in fright.

Charity rummaged for her rifle in the pile of goods to one side, while Peter hurriedly dressed and produced his six-gun. "We've got to fire at them, scare them away," he advised. "Turn the leaders and the rest is easy."

"Zelda, Charlie, all of you," Charity shouted over the tumult. "If you have any weapons, get them and shoot into the air, over the cattle's heads."

Already she stood at the tailgate, flame and noise spitting from her Marlin Pacific rifle. Peter joined her. Cattle seemed to be everywhere. In the distance they could her thin voices shouting and see the occasional flash of a muzzle blast. More horns could be seen, bodies and horns flickering jerkily in the actinic glare of the lightning. More rain fell, obscuring everything for a moment. A loud crash and the sound of wood splintering sent a stab of fear to Charity's heart.

Terrified shrieks followed. The black night split open with a searing glare of white light, and Charity saw the shattered remains of the other wagon buffeted by a steady flow of cattle, their legs moving weirdly in the pulsing light. Tatters of the canvas cover flapped madly in the howling wind. As quickly as it had come, the illumination cut off, a seething deluge drumming down from heaven.

"Keep it up," Peter urged. "It's the only hope we've got."

"How much chance is there?" Charity asked over the raging storm.

Sadness and a tinge of fear washed over Peter's face. "To tell the truth, not much. We have to turn them, Charity."

All through the night the battle raged against stampede and storm. With morning's hazy, overcast light, some relief came. The ferocity of the storm abated, winding down to a slow, regular downpour. Gone were the violent winds, hail, rain and lightning of the night. The ground around the tarts' encampment had a covering of dead animals. Many jack rabbits, some quail and a number of blown-apart steers, dead horses and, to everyone's horror, human bodies littered the sodden ground. It had taken all night to turn the herd; it had still not stopped moving, though the panic had left it. Most of the drovers remained out, seeking strays and fighting the elements to bring them back to the restless gather. Mud, animal carcasses and splintered wood littered the unhappy camp of the sisters of sin and their benefactor, Charity Rose.

Sorrowful weeping rose from the huddled young women. Their sodden clothing clung tightly as they gathered around two still forms lying on portions of broken wagon box. The pounding hoofs of the cattle had nearly destroyed any identifiable features, the chests caved in, limbs trampled. There would have to be a burial of sorts, Charity considered, for Adrianne and Clarisse. The trail crew had suffered losses also, she had learned less than an hour after sunup.

Peter Norton rode over to learn how the ladies had fared and to inform them that one drover had been trampled to death by the stampede, while three others suffered broken fingers, an arm, and a leg, with several more receiving sprains and strains.

"It'll take," he estimated, "three days to collect in the strays and calm the herd enough for the last leg of the drive. Uh, Mister Dalton said to let you know, those who can will come for the funeral service. If it's no trouble, he'd like to bring our dead to bury."

"Of course you can, Peter," Charity responded absently, her heart heavy.

It was a far different encounter from that of the previous night. Solemn and reserved, the girls showed none of their former lascivious behavior, and the rowdy, lustful manner had deserted the drovers. When the graves had been dug, everyone gathered around and placed the blanket-wrapped bodies into the ground. The girls wept quietly and the solemn-faced cowboys shuffled their feet uncomfortably, hats off and held in front of them. Grover Dalton produced a small, gold-edged Bible from a voluminous coat pocket and opened it.

"I'm not much at this, but I'll do the best I can. 'The Lord giveth and the Lord taketh away,'" he intoned. "'Ashes to ashes, and dust to dust. Lord, into Your keeping we commit these, Thy servants, Margaret Dimwittie, known to us as Clarisse, Mildred Osborne, known to us as Adrianne, and Clarence Baxter, a bachelor cowboy, with the sure and constant hope for the resurrection of the dead and the life everlasting. Amen.'"

Six drovers began to shovel dirt and stones into the graves. Dalton returned the Bible to his pocket and walked over to where Charity stood.

"What do you plan to do now?"

"There's not much that can be done," Charity answered him. "The girls lost most of their finery in the stampede. We've only one wagon. Thanks to you, your men found our horses and returned them. We'll just . . . move on deeper into Kansas, I suppose."

"You're a brave woman, Miss Charity," Dalton allowed. "I've had Taters bring some supplies; some flour, bacon, beans, coffee. I only wish I could do something more for you."

"That's more than generous, Mister Dalton. Your kindness will be greatly appreciated. We'll be able to manage. I only hope that—somehow I can find these girls some better form of work when we reach Dodge City."

Dalton cracked a bit of a smile. "Whatever you arrange, we'll probably see you there. Now we've a lot of nervous cows to tend to. Good-bye, Miss Charity."

"Good-bye, Mister Dalton. You're a true gentleman."

"Sunday's the day," Bat Masterson informed the collection of gunfighters arranged around a large deal table in the Fossett and Dunlap Saloon in Ingalls, Kansas. "Everything will be closed and the folks in church. Them that aren't will still be suffering from the effects of Saturday night's revelry. We ride in with a spring wagon, load up the county paraphernalia and skinny on out with no one the wiser. How's that sound?"

"Uh . . . *risky* the answer you want, Bat?" Billy Tilghman joked.

"C'mon, Bill. You helped me scout out that phony courthouse they have set up in Cimarron. You know how easy it'll be," Bat prompted.

"Sure. And I know that what we're doin' is legal, 'cause the Supreme Court ruled that Ingalls is the county seat. All the same, there's been a little shootin' around here, and I hear some folks down Crowley County way got killed over a like deal," Tilghman answered. "Chances are you've got the best plan, Bat."

"Then that's the way we'll work it," Jim Marshall put in. "I've got a hankerin' to end this thing damned soon."

"Someone been walkin' over your grave, Jim?" Masterson asked archly.

"Uh, no, but . . ." Marshall let his words drift away and sat stroking his white goatee.

"That's what we all want, Jim," Masterson assured him. "The same for Mr. Soule and the folks in Ingalls. You are I are supposed to go in and get all the records. Billy, George, Ed, the rest of you, will wait with the wagon. Simple enough if we work quickly."

"So you say," Fred Singer interjected in a sour tone. "I've yet to see one of these things go perfect."

"We took the wrong road," Zelda observed when the wagon halted beside the small sign that identified the community as Cimarron, Kansas.

Astride Lucifer, Charity Rose wiped her brow and forced a smile. "For right now, a town is a town. We can go on to Dodge City later."

Charity might well have debated the wisdom of stopping in Cimarron, had she the gift of foresight. The small community basked in the Kansas sun, warming toward a hot, humid afternoon. Horses and wagons crowded the main thoroughfare, tied off before stores and saloons. The central intersection held an octagonal bandstand made of lath and painted white. A flagpole and windmill shared space with the entertainment center of the town. When the bedraggled cavalcade stopped before the hotel, Charity dismounted and quietly admonished her wards.

"Remember to register under your real names. None of this Fleur LaDux foolishness, Zelda," Charity commanded. "That goes for the rest of you. And try to act like . . . other than your calling."

Inside the girls signed and paid for their rooms. It took most of the money they salvaged after the stampede. At once, they began complaining about it to Charity. She raised a hand to silence them and looked over her charges, angry, yet touched by their absolute trust and dependence on her.

"All right, girls. Once we get settled in and cleaned up some, we'll go shopping. You need new things, that's for certain."

"Oh, yes," Charlie replied. "We won't be able to work without them. I wonder if they'll have my size tights?"

A tittering waterfall of giggles went the rounds. Red-faced, Charity snapped back, "I wasn't thinking of exactly that sort of clothing."

"What else, honey?" Evette asked with a straight face. "If we're gonna get work and recover our losses."

Word made the rounds rapidly after that exchange, from the gossipy hotel clerk and the wagging tongues of the haberdasher and milliner to the clacking disapproval of the gimlet-eyed guardians of local morality: A madam and her string of harlots had invaded their fair community. The majority held with this consensus and viewed their comings and goings with jaundiced eyes.

"You say you wish appointments for seven women to have their hair trimmed and styled?" a cold-eyed woman with a tiny rosebud mouth and too-round cheeks repeated back to Charity. "With matching falls and rats made from the excess? I'm so sorry, but I'm booked up until way late next week. Perhaps then, dear?"

"Thank you, no. But I would like to buy a variety of chignons," Charity returned frigidly.

She set the bevy of doves to washing, cutting and styling each other's hair. They also did seamstress work, since the alterations lady claimed she had her time booked way into the next month. Charity discovered that her brood had performed similar tasks in numerous bordellos in the past. They seemed quite content with it, so she left them to their work. On the morning of their second day in Cimarron, the town marshal paid a call on Charity in her room.

"If you're lookin' to set up a dance hall in Cimarron, you've come to the wrong town," the bitter-mouthed, mustachioed marshal clipped sharply.

"Oh, quite the contrary, Marshal. I'm seeking to find suitable, honest employment for these young ladies."

Marshal Trask cocked a dubious eyebrow. "Oh? Such as what?"

"Well, they'd hardly make proper schoolteachers," Charity admitted frankly. "Yet they have the same maternal instincts as any woman and could be fine nurses and caretakers for children, shop clerks, perhaps operate an eating house."

"Hummmph! You can't change the spots on an old dog," the lawman observed. "Meanin', you've got a passel of harlots there and we've got more than enough around town already. Best be figurin' on movin' on." He rose to leave.

"I'll keep that in mind, Marshal. Thank you for your advice."

"I'd be for followin' it, were I you," Trask snapped on his way to the door.

Sunday morning dawned warm and humid. The aroma of sage, burdock and columbine perfumed the damp air. Shortly after dawn, Bat Masterson, Billy Tilghman, Jim Marshall, George Bolds, Ed Brooks, Neal Brown and Fred Singer departed from Ingalls in a spring wagon. Ben Daniels, Eat 'Em Up Jake, and George and John Gilbert accompanied them on horseback. Their short ride to Cimarron proved uneventful. True to Masterson's prediction, the roisterers nursed hangovers indoors, while the faithful filled the community's churches. Only an occasional idler could be found on the boardwalks of the downtown district.

"Pull it on up in front, Neal," Masterson instructed.

Once the spring wagon stopped at the courthouse, Masterson and veteran peace officer Jim Marshall climbed down, straightened their long black coats and walked up the native limestone steps to the front door of the Cimarron county offices. Bat Masterson swung the tall golden oak panels wide and strolled inside. There he and Marshall discovered County Clerk A. T. Riley seated at his desk. He looked up from the documents spread before him with surprise and inquired haltingly, "Wh-what are you gentlemen doing here?"

Thinking fast, Bat fired back, "We might ask you the same thing."

"Why, I—I'm putting in a little overtime to catch up on the records. This constant wrangle over the location of the county seat has left the files in terrible order."

Masterson's hand moved with a blur as he produced a six-gun. Marshall did the same. "Speaking of that, you can oblige us by turning over those books right now."

"Yee-yer from Ingalls!" Riley squeaked.

"That's right. We've come to get what rightfully belongs there," Jim Marshall informed the astounded clerk. He held his revolver on Riley while Masterson strode to the door.

"You boys can come in now and start loadin' this stuff," Bat commanded. "We're going to check on the upstairs."

Within two minutes, ledgers, record journals and account books began to form an untidy pile in the spring wagon. Along the block a ways, residents of Cimarron gawked in disbelief, then reacted with indignation and alarm. Quickly they spread the word while the raiders tossed bundles of documents into the wagon bed. Within five minutes, Cimarron suddenly woke up to the fact that it was being stripped of its claim to county-seatdom.

While Masterson and Marshall toiled on the records upstairs, a crowd of several hundred armed and indignant men swiftly gathered around the courthouse. Angry words were exchanged with the looters, and the shooting started. Bullets clipped through clothing and smacked against the limestone front of the courthouse.

"My God, I'm hit!" George Bolds cried out.

"Me, too," Fred Singer added.

"Let's get out of here," Bill Tilghman advised.

The men in the wagon took off in a withering lash of lead, leaving Masterson and Marshall stranded on the second floor. They had no alternative but to flee, Bat Masterson acknowledged.

"Although they could have delayed a moment or two longer to let us join them," he observed sourly to Jim Marshall.

"Looks like we're up agin' it, Bat," Marshall opined.

"We've got to stand them off, Jim, or our lives will get spent far too cheaply," Bat summed up.

A maelstrom of lead shattered windows and kept them low. The two besieged men worked hard to put up a stout defense. Three of the bolder among the Cimarron faction attempted to rush the stairs, only to retreat under blazingly accurate fire. An hour passed and matters quieted some. One of the Cimmaron men who helped lay siege took off his hat and found a bullet had pierced its crown. He felt closely of his head and discovered the slug had clipped a lock of his hair.

"Ain't you scared?" a grizzled oldster nearby inquired.

"Oh, hell yes. If my hair hadn't been standing on end, it wouldn't have got shot off that way."

Charity Rose, Charlie Cramer and Tina Lewis left the hotel early to get some breakfast that Sunday morning. They'd no sooner seated themselves in a corner café and ordered coffee than a tinkling sound came from the upper portion of the large front window, followed by a solid smack as a bullet entered and struck the plaster wall. A veritable fusillade followed.

"Wha-what is it?" Tina asked in a small, frightened voice.

"I think we're in some sort of battle," Charity observed.

"Damned Ingalls fellers," a man complained, entering the diner to reload his revolver. "They've done sent those gunfighters over here."

"What's the reason for that?" Charity asked firmly.

"They're tryin' to steal the county seat," came the reply.

The standoff continued for more than an hour. Fed now and growing restive, the three young women began to see the café as some sort of confinement. They wanted to go out, but dreaded doing so. Another hour passed and the firing increased once more. At last Charity gathered her purse, paid the bill and rose to depart.

"War or no war, we have to get out of here," she declared.

"Oh, Charity, what if we're—we're gunned down?" Tina wailed in a whisper.

"They'll not do that to us, I can assure you," Charity answered with more confidence than she felt. "All we have to do is walk down the block to the hotel. We'll be safe enough."

Another bullet crashed noisily through the big window. "Are you sure?" Charlie asked timidly.

Chapter Fourteen

Out on the boardwalk, Charity and her companions got a good look at the siege activity. Men with rifles, shotguns and revolvers stood along the building fronts and circled the courthouse. Periodically they would loose a few dozen rounds, then settle back. Charity shepherded her charges along the wooden sidewalk.

They had walked some thirty yards, a good block from the courthouse, when the man standing beside Charity, his hands in his pockets, ignoring the lopsided siege, suddenly fell dead, a bullet through his head. Immediately Tina began to wail and, choking, lost her breakfast.

"You call this *safe enough?*" Charlie demanded.

"Look-a there," a man growled, pointing to the newly made corpse.

"We oughtta hang 'em when we get 'em out," the burly fellow with him remarked. "Who's in there, anyway?"

"Masterson and Marshall from Dodge City," came the reply from a third townsman.

"Oh, shit, they're mighty good," the inquirer observed.

"Don't matter," growled the beefy citizen. "When an' if

we can root 'em out, we oughtta build us a couple of hemp collars."

Charity gritted her teeth and steered Charlie and Tina past the fallen Cimarronian.

Upstairs in the courthouse, Jim Marshall turned away from a window and began reloading. "Looks like they're fixin' to stay a while, Bat."

"Only too likely, Jim," Bat acknowledged.

"String 'em up!" a voice called from below.

"Get 'em outta there and hang th' murderin' sons-a-bitches," another took up.

"Don't sound like surrendering would be too good an idea," Marshall offered.

"What are they talking about?" Bat asked of no one. "Who's been murdered?"

"Maybe if we can hold out long enough they'll cool down," Jim suggested.

"We'd better hope so," Masterson added fervently.

Through the afternoon and night, the doughty gunfighters stood off the entire town. Charity and her doves watched on, with little else to do. Several of the more hardened girls speculated, then offered wagers on whether or when the pair of sharpshooters would be driven from the courthouse or killed. Charity thought it revolting. Speculation ran high, though, and before long there were gentlemen to take those bets. After nightfall, when the saloons opened again, the spirits flowed, along with tempers.

"Burn 'em out, I say," one Cimarron booster announced.

"Sure. Wipe out our nice new courthouse to do it, eh?"

"We won't be needin' a courthouse if they get away with

this stunt," came the surly reply.

A flurry of shots broke up the confrontation before blows were exchanged. An excited voice called from down the street, "They're tryin' to sneak out the back way!"

"Get around there," came another bull roar.

Charity, along with Evette, Charlie and Tina, tried to maintain some degree of decorum while they dined in the cut-rate luxury of the hotel dining room. The menu made up for the cut glass instead of crystal, crockery stoneware rather than china and faded, molting flocked wallpaper.

"Roast prairie hen," Tina enthused. "Sounds delicious."

"I love beef tongue," Evette confided. "I do hope this buffalo is as good."

Charity studied the list of vegetables. Creamed onions, potatoes au gratin, glazed carrots and collard greens seemed more than adequate to grace the whole fried catfish she had ordered. She'd sample the tongue and prairie chicken as well, she felt certain. For dessert, she noticed, they listed cherry cobbler, gooseberry pie and rum cake. Oh, well, she thought lightly. If she had room.

After such a repast, everyone felt logy. They retired early, though random gunshots kept disturbing their slumber. Monday morning dawned clouded and chill. Masterson and Marshall remained in the courthouse. Breakfast tasted like fried cardboard on sleepy palates. Charity suggested they begin to pack their new clothing and make ready to leave.

"Why now?" Charlie protested. "We don't know what's gonna happen."

"Charlie's right," Zelda added. "That's two of the most famous shootists in the country over in the courthouse and we're right in place to see how it comes out."

"For one thing, the men I'm after wouldn't be caught sight of in the same county with lawmen like Bat Masterson and Billy Tilghman. They're wanted from the Red River to the Colorado. Concho Bill Baudine's not yellow, but he isn't stupid either. I saw in the morning newspaper that there's another county-seat war in Crowley County. My bet is that Baudine's there. I'll see you girls to Dodge City and then turn southeast to Crowley."

"No, please," Tina begged. "Take us with you. We don't know what to do, how to act."

"Start packing," Charity stated sternly.

Shortly before noon, another blaze of gunfire alerted the whole town. It died off when Bat Masterson removed the stiff-front white shirt he wore and waved it out the window. Their ammunition exhausted, the shootist pair decided on surrender as the only course.

"Hang 'em high!" a tall, lean man with a granite jaw and cold, steely eyes called from where he leaned against a support post in front of the saloon.

"Awh, why hang 'em?" a portly businessman inquired of the crowd. "For a few dollars more, we could have hired them."

"I've got a fistful of dollars says they'll swing before the day's over," the rugged stranger announced.

"Now see here, Mister . . ." the storekeeper protested. "Say, I didn't get your name."

"That's right, you didn't," answered the stranger as he turned and stalked off in a cloud of smoke from his long, thin cheroot.

"This is a good time for us to be going," Charity advised the doves, who flocked to the windows of their rooms.

"We've got to collect on our bets," Evette reminded her.

"You can do that downstairs. The clerk's holding them, isn't he? I say we go."

Wheedling protests answered her until interrupted by

the commotion down the street. "Hang 'em now, I say," an angry citizen of Cimarron demanded. "Right here in front of the courthouse."

"That's as good a reason to go as I can think of," Charity informed the girls.

A shot blasted over the clamorings for rope and a quick death. "Who's that?" Zelda asked.

"I don't know," Charity responded.

"Hey, Sheriff, let us alone," someone complained, answering their question.

"Yeah, we want to hang these men."

"You'll not do that," the sheriff countered. "They're my prisoners and they'll stand trial for murder. Now clear the way. I'm taking them to jail."

Amid many grumbles and halfhearted threats, he carried out his intentions. Charity nodded toward the street.

"Those people are going to get ugly. That's why we make tracks."

At last Zelda, Nichole and Evette saw the sense of it.

At least they didn't look like refugees from a flood, Charity compared gratefully as she and her brood entered the moderate-sized community of Hopewell, Kansas. They rode along a tree-lined street to the center of town. Barefoot children ran laughing over the dirt ruts, splashing brown sprays from the occasional puddles. A holiday atmosphere pervaded the business district. Across from the general mercantile, at the *Hopewell Clarion,* a man in shirtsleeves and a green eyeshade posted the front page of a newspaper in the largest, center pane of a bay window.

HOPEWELL UPHELD AS COUNTY SEAT!

Below the banner headline, a subhead declared:

Kansas Supreme Court Verifies Ballot Count

"It looks like we may have gotten here too late," Zelda stated smugly.

"The Supreme Court had verified Ingalls as county seat, too," Charity reminded her. "I wouldn't be surprised if we got here right in the middle of it. Looks like we have our pick of hotels," she added, changing the subject.

The eight newcomers checked in at the Ransom Hotel. Charity had to jab Tina in the ribs to keep her from signing the register as Monique Flobert. This time she had to dig into her own reserve of cash to pay for their rooms. The girls had lost more bets than they had won. Gambling, as Zelda put it, was not their game. Charity added enough for a bath each, and she and Zelda took the livestock to the livery stable. With the usual dispatch of small towns, the intelligence of their arrival made the rounds within an hour.

"It's disgraceful," Amanda Bittles declared over a table littered with pastry remains and used coffee cups.

Doughty Mildred Taller studied the buxom, formidable figure of the mayor's wife and nodded her agreement. She wetted thin lips, which she constantly pursed in disapproval of the world she observed, and spoke in a reedy, nasal tone.

"What is your husband doing about it, Amanda? After all, ten drabs descended in our midst all at once. Bad enough we have to helplessly stand by and allow the presence of half a dozen or so in those horrible saloons."

"Mildred is right, Amanda," put in a broom-thin, gaunt-faced woman with an overlarge head on a long stalk of scrawny neck. "Think of the moral climate that makes for our children."

"I can't agree with you more, Hannah," Amanda Bittles responded. "I haven't had the time to talk to Jeremy about it as yet. I only learned of this happening on my way here for our weekly meeting. This is the sort of ugly, immoral situation for which we founded the Decency League. To contend with evil is our motto. I feel we should call on Leonard Ransom at the hotel and suggest he might find it necessary to limit their stay to a single night."

"Yes," Hannah Noonan said brightly. "Compel them to move on. And I think we should hold a public meeting tomorrow afternoon to condemn sin. I'll bring my bass drum."

"I'll have my tambourine and cornet ready," Rheba Classen prompted.

Swept up by it, Amanda Bittles added her share. "Black skirts, white waist-shirts with plain ruffles. Our black hats and veils. Mildred, can we count on you to make some placards?"

Breathless with excitement, Mildred Taller blurted, "Certainly, Amanda. I have some left from our last campaign at election time. Also, I can put Stevie and Melissa on to doing more. They're always after me for something to do when there's no school."

"Excellent," Amanda concluded. "Be sure to tell everyone. We can have quite a time of it. Now, who wants to come with me to see Leonard?"

Most of the men of Hopewell saw the recent event in a somewhat different light. The older among them examined the bevy of feminine beauty with wistful remembrance. The younger evaluated their presence with naked lust. None received news of the situation with indifference. Even small boys shied sneaky glances in the direction of the crowded wagon of tasteful tarts in hopes of catching a glimpse of bare leg up a windblown skirt.

Although this was far more cordial than their welcome in Cimarron, Charity nevertheless felt the pressure of ostricism.

"We're going to have trouble with the ladies of this town," she predicted to the seven sisters of sin. "I noticed three businesses that removed Help Wanted signs from their windows when we rode in this morning."

"Well," Monique-Tina suggested, "we could always go back to our old trade."

"That's what they're all expecting," Charity answered her. "Tomorrow, we set out to find all of you some sort of work, and to learn what we can about the county-seat feud."

They learned little and received no job offers. Dejected and feeling unwanted, the soiled doves gathered in Charity's room following the evening meal the next day. Other than what they had all read in the newspaper story, they had gathered no specific knowledge of the contest between nearby Cottonwood Springs and Hopewell.

"We should have gone to Dodge City," Nichole complained.

"I offered to take you there first. My business is here. Or at least I think it is," Charity returned.

Despite her efforts, three of the girls slipped away from the hotel and plied the trade in the Four Aces Saloon. Their simple, modest dresses seemed to excite the patrons more than the usual gaudy costumes. They had no difficulty in arranging to satiate a half-dozen customers each.

The cocks had crowed the morning awake when Charity came down for breakfast. Seventy dollars in gold weighed down her purse, the girls' earnings of the previous night less five dollars each for personal expenses. It embarrassed her, yet she rationalized it as compensation for their lodging and meals. Unprepared for the wealth of information, now suddenly delivered to her, she went unobserved by those discussing the latest events.

"Ve barely got away vit our lives," Otto Blutcher informed the hotel proprietor, Aaron Barlow. "My vife, here, got to hiccoughing and I thought ve'd be heard by Baudine's night guards."

"I can't believe a whole town has been taken over by outlaws, Otto," Barlow stated flatly. "Why, what happened to your marshal? The mayor and town council?"

"Baudine gunned down the marshal and the mayor. Then his men disarmed ef'ryone. Th-the folks are prisoners in their own town."

"Did you see Sheriff Meadows?" Barlow asked.

"*Ja*. And he didn't seem too concerned about doing anything."

"What did he say, Otto?"

"He told me that a town that vent to hiring gunfighters ought to expect something like that, Aaron. Said he didn't have the firepower necessary to do anything about it."

"Well, I suppose," Barlow went on with a shrug.

When their conversation ended, Charity approached the desk. "I would like to pay for a week's stay, keeping the rooms we have now."

"Well now, I, ah . . ." Aaron Barlow stammered, mindful of the visit by Amanda Bittles to the owner, Leonard Ransom.

"That would come to twenty-eight dollars, with another eight for baths. I'll be paying in gold," Charity went on undisturbed.

"Er, ah, gold? Well, then, ah . . ." Barlow cleared his throat roughly. "I'm certain we can accommodate you, Miss Rose. Yes, indeed." He'd deal with Leonard and Amanda later, Aaron concluded.

"Thank you so much," Charity said sweetly. When

she'd paid and received a receipt, she turned to Otto Blutcher. "Mister Blutcher, I couldn't help overhearing your conversation. As it happens, I'm interested in a man named Baudine. Would the man cowing your town happen to be named Concho Bill Baudine?"

Blutcher scowled blackly at the mention of the name. "*Ja*. Thats the vun. Vy do you want anything to do vit him?"

"I intend to capture him for the reward," Charity answered coldly. "Preferably dead."

"Don't pay any attention to her, Otto," Aaron Barlow stated as he approached, making shooing motions with his long, pallid fingers.

"Just why is that, Mister, ah, Barlow?" Charity demanded icily.

To Blutcher, the hotelier explained, "She's the, ah, proprietress of a traveling, ah, bordello." To Charity he spoke nastily. "A woman in your position is no doubt far more familiar with outlaws like this Baudine. That doesn't, however, qualify you to attempt getting a reward."

Bits and pieces of this seemingly universal prejudice at last built to an unbearable peak within Charity's consciousness, and she came back angrily, "For the last time. I *am not* a madam and they are not *my* girls. I came here to collect the bounty on Bill Baudine and as many of his men as I have papers on. I'm carrying a Special Deputy badge from the Havupai County, Arizona Territory sheriff's office."

"Sure. And traveling with a bunch of whores," a new voice joined in as Mayor Bittles entered through the tall, narrow, etched-glass front doors.

Completely at a loss, Otto Blutcher slumped down into a red plush wing chair, head resting on the white antimacassar, pudgy hands covering his face.

"Oh, hello, Jeremy," Barlow said in a flustered state. "Your wife was here yesterday . . ."

"And I'm here today."

"I was about to give them notice now," Barlow went on, ignoring the mayor's interruption.

"Very good, Aaron. See that you do."

"Notice of what?" Charity demanded.

"Th-that this must be your last . . . last day. There are rules, an-and laws regarding the keeper of a disorderly house using a hotel for business purposes."

Affronted, her Irish temper fully aroused, Charity snapped back, "We've done no such thing!"

Barlow waggled a long, thin index finger under her nose, a nasty sneer of triumph spoiling his features. "Three of you did last night. A regular parade through here. Two by two. You'd think Noah had built this place."

Oh, damn. She'd forgotten about that. Chagrined, Charity tried to put a better front on it. "That was expressly against my wishes. What matters is that I have paid for a week's lodging and have a receipt, which constitutes a contract. We're staying."

"You could get into a lot of trouble this way," Mayor Bittles threatened darkly.

"Oh no, not I. It's the owner of this establishment who could get into trouble. I'll handle the girls and guarantee nothing like that will happen again. What's important now is to get a posse organized and deal with Concho Bill Baudine."

"You'll not get a posse gathered here to ride to the relief of Cottonwood Springs," Sheriff Meadows informed her half an hour later. "Those people have stolen the records and ledgers twice during our fight over the county seat. Now there's a boy missing from here and a

U.S. Marshal that's not come back."

Charity developed a grim expression. "That sounds like Concho Bill's doing. All the more reason to act quickly, Sheriff."

"You're talking about an easy way to get a lot of innocent, inexperienced people killed, miss. Until I can relay Mister Blutcher's information on to the state authorities, we'll do nothing to create more difficulties with whoever is doing these things in Cottonwood Springs."

"If you won't, Sheriff, then I will," Charity snapped. Before any response could be made, she turned sharply on one heel and stalked out of the sheriff's office.

Chapter Fifteen

Smoky twilight entered the room of the Cottonwood Springs hotel when Willie Hansen burst in with news for Concho Bill. He seemed excited and pleased at one time. His words soon explained it.

"Dandy Spencer's come in with his boys, Bill," he exclaimed.

"Well, well, well, Dandy Spencer," Baudine mused. "I've not seen that big ox in a coon's age. Who all'd he bring with him?"

"Monroe, an' that crazy brother of his, Will," Hansen listed. "Bobby, that one they call the Fargo Kid, an' Wild Mike, an' a fancy-dressed feller they call Reno. An' a couple of fellers I don't know. They're all bellied up over at the Red Garter."

"Wouldn't be polite not going over to welcome them, I suppose. Keep an eye on that Monroe, though. I've heard tell that no one's ever gotten every gun he carries off him."

"You figure they'll make some trouble for us, Bill?" Hansen asked.

"No. Ol' Dandy's just come in to take advantage of our hospitality. Dandy makes the third top dog to bring his boys in with us. Might be we can even set up a job or two for all of us to work on. Come on, Frenchy, join us. You haven't seen Dandy in a few years, either."

"*Mais oui*. He is, as you say, one big one."

In the Ransom Hotel, Charity selected what she would take with care and packed in tense silence. It didn't take her charges long to learn of her intentions. Zelda, Charlie, Evette and Tina came to her room, worry for her rather than themselves motivating them for once.

"Honey, what do you mean you go'n take on all those outlaws by yo'self?" Evette demanded, hands on hips. Her eyes had grown large and round, and she cocked her head to one side as though chiding a small child.

"I'll not stand aside because some lawman has lost his nerve. Especially when he refuses me any aid because everyone thinks I am . . . I'm a *madam!*" In an unaccustomed gesture, Charity stamped her foot.

Tears formed in Tina's eyes. "Oh, Charity, it's all our fault. If you didn't have us around, maybe—maybe they'd listen."

"I won't say you're wrong," Charity replied in a kindly tone. "But it's a lot more than that. Men . . . just won't listen to a woman. Even if she's right. Particularly when it comes to such matters as this. We've only one course to resort to."

"Two, honey," Evette corrected. "There's tears, of course. An' we can cut off their supply. Like those Greek women in that story I read—*Lysistrata*."

"Actually there's three," Helen Moran said gruffly from the open doorway. "We can always bitch at them until we drive them to distraction."

"Well then, I'm fairly well armed," Charity observed lightly. "If only we had time enough to use those methods. As it is, I'm committed. I've come this far and I'm going to be in on the end."

"We won't let you go," Charlie and Evette chorused.

"Not unless we go, too," Zelda and Helen stated firmly.

"What nonsense is this?" Charity demanded, shaking a finger at them. "Why, you wouldn't have a chance. You don't know the first thing . . . Baudine and his gang are dangerous killers. How did you ever come up with . . ." On and on, the arguments rolled from Charity.

Zelda and the soiled doves listened silently, faces noncommittal, until she ran down. Then, eyes alight, expressions avid with an odd sort of what might be kill lust, they presented wild, unworkable schemes.

"They'd never suspect us," Zelda offered. "We could get right in among them and start shooting before they had a chance."

"Top shootists like Baudine leads would cut you to pieces," Charity countered.

"We could pretend to be, ah, well, what we are and get their trust. Then poison them all," Tina suggested, with a peculiar sort of glee on her face.

"Too risky," Charity answered plainly. "Besides, men would hang *us* for that."

"We could just watch and listen and report back to the sheriff," Helen proposed. "Sooner or later he'd *have* to do something."

"That makes some sense," Charity allowed.

"Get 'em in bed, then kill 'em all in their sleep," Penelope advised with bloodthirsty relish.

"We're only eight," Charity said, appealing to reason. "There's at least twenty of them. Do you think we could get them to die in shifts?"

When all the proposals had been offered and rejected, the disheartened ladies lapsed into silence. Charity tightened the straps on her pack pouches and considered what these ostracized women had been willing to sacrifice. A twinge of conscience pierced her heart. This was not bravado, she understood only too well. All of them wanted to help. They seemed aware enough of potential dangers, and willing to use any means, some of them terrible in their extremity, to bring down the outlaws. In the end, did she have the right to refuse them a chance to aid her?

"Can any of you shoot?" Charity inquired with a sigh.

Eagerness painted the doves' faces. They all tried to answer at once. Charlie managed to rise above the rest.

"I can. Poppa taught me to shoot when I was seven. I'm good, too, with a rifle or shotgun."

"I have a derringer I can hit with up to twelve feet or so," Helen informed Charity. "I'm fair to middlin' with a thirty-two–twenty revolver."

"I've never used a gun," Nichole admitted apologetically, "but I'm willing to learn."

"Enough, enough," Charity appealed, hands held out for silence.

"All right, you've convinced me. If you apply yourselves, learn how to handle guns, dynamite, knives and the other tools of the trade in a week's time, you can come along. We can't take the wagon along, so you'll have to learn to ride horseback—astraddle, not in a side-rig. And you'll have to toughen yourselves. We'll do a lot of running, exercises to strengthen your wrists and arms, increase your reflexes. If you're willing, and do all that within a week, we might have a chance."

Zelda threw her arms around Charity's neck and gave her a big hug. "Oh, Charity, we're going to help you. We'll get those owlhoots, I know we will."

Charity answered her with a crooked, decidedly uncertain smile.

Outside, a bass drum began to thump, and a cornet added its brassy voice.

" 'When the ro-o-oll is called up yon-der, I'lllll be there.' " With a final bang and clash of cymbals, the hymn ended. "*A—men.*"

Amanda Bittles, chubby hands on ample, black-clad hips, surveyed the scant collection of the curious and the inevitable loungers who gawked at her Decency League sisters. They stood in the dust at the center of the intersection closest to the Ransom Hotel. A hot sun beat relentlessly down on their black hats and caused freshets of perspiration to flow along the sides of their uniformly flushed faces. Droplets fell from the prominent, sharp tip of Hannah Noonan's nose.

"Friends," Amanda began in a hearty bellow. "Citizens of Hopewell. We come in the name of decency. And decency demands that we confront a scandal so heinous that its very name needs never befoul the lips of morally upright, righteous-living womankind. When Adam first corrupted Eve in the Garden, the seeds were sewn to blacken all mankind. Now our fair community is visited by a veritable horde of the sisters of perdition. *We must not tolerate it!* Cast them out! Turn to them your backs in righteous wrath and send them forth chastised and branded with the mark of their sin. Have no mercy! Cast them forth from our midst. Now we will sing 'Blood of the Lamb.' "

"She's talking about us," Nichole remarked with a pout.

"No doubt about that," Charity agreed.

Eyes alight with an odd fire, Charlie stepped past her sisters and walked out onto the narrow balcony overlooking the street. At her appearance, many spectators looked upward. "Ooohs" and "Aaaahs" came in a low mutter, and several waggled fingers at her.

Although she shook with anger, Charlie extended one

arm, her finger pointed at the rotund matron who had spoken.

"It says in Matthew, the sixth chapter . . ." Now the musicians had ceased and everyone stared toward Charlie. " 'Therefore . . . do not sound a trumpet before thee, as the hypocrites do in the synagogues and in the streets, that they may have glory of men.' And later it says in the fifth verse of that chapter, 'And when thou prayest, thou shalt not be as the hypocrites are: for they love to pray standing . . . in the corners of the streets, that they may be seen of men.' Where does that put you, lady?" Smiling sweetly, Charlie remained an unmoving rebuke to the zealots of the League below.

"A Bible-quoting harlot!" Amanda Bittles gasped that evening at the dinner table. "Who ever heard of such a thing?"

"Darn few, I reckon," her husband, Jeremy, replied with a tolerant chuckle as he laid aside his fork and pushed back his pie plate. "But she sure plucked a rose off you, now didn't she?"

"Jeremy, are you taking the side of those—those *jades?*" Amanda threatened.

"Oh, no, my dear. Not at all. Only observing that the one, brazen as she may be, certainly has a flair for debate. And that young lady traveling with them is not their, ah, keeper so's to speak; rather, she's a female bounty hunter."

"Even more scandalous and degrading," Amanda snapped. "What is the world coming to when women sink to such low callings?"

"Women have been selling their, ah, favors since time immemorial, my dear," Jeremy told his wife in an offhand manner.

"I'm not talking about that," Amanda's anger-tinged voice grated out. "What else have you ferreted out about these blights on the face of fair womanhood?"

"Can you imagine? This, ah, Charity Rose is undertaking to train the ladies of ill repute in the arts of fighting. It appears they plan some sort of action against the outlaws in Cottonwood Springs."

"Th-the very idea!" Amanda squeaked, outraged.

"Yes . . . isn't it?" Jeremy answered back calmly.

Concho Bill Baudine didn't wait for retribution to be trained and led against him. Unaware of the proximity and intent of Charity Rose, he acceded to the wishes of Karl Richter and rode out with a dozen men to deliver from the rightful county courthouse in Hopewell the county records so assiduously desired by the men who had engaged them. So doing, Richter assured them, would aim in winning the goodwill of Cottonwood Springs residents. Their journey went without incident.

Shortly after midnight, Concho Bill stopped at the side of the Hopewell courthouse and gestured to his men. "Dan, Owen, you and Hal come with me. We'll go in and relieve these yokels of the records. When you bring 'em out, stuff 'em into saddlebags."

"Me, too, huh, Bill?" Tiny Jim Boyle inquired eagerly.

"You stay here, Tiny Jim. I don't want you stumbling into anything and raising an alarm."

"Awh, Bill . . ."

"No nonsense now, Jim, hear me?"

In half an hour the job had been completed. Quiet as ghosts, the outlaws drifted out of town, headed away from Cottonwood Springs. They would use a circuitous route in order to throw off any pursuit.

Dawn brought an explosion of indignation and rage

among the varying interests in Hopewell.

"They've done it again!" Hiram Weeks shouted from the steps of the looted courthouse. "Damn them Springers!"

Over at the *Clarion*, the editor shook his head sadly, though he could not squelch the cynical grin that spread on his face.

"Ladies, this is the Colt double-action Lightning, Model Eighty-two revolver," Charity informed her seven recruits. "It has a loading gate in the same position as the single-action Frontier models, and is equipped with an ejection rod. This particular model is in thirty-eight Colt caliber. There is little recoil and less muzzle flash than larger-bore weapons."

Early morning sunlight fractured into myriad shards of twinkling highlights from an acre of broken glass. At the south end of town, the male residents of Hopewell had set up an informal target range, which had accounted for many an empty whiskey bottle and colored glass ball "pigeon" in contests of the past. Charity and the doves now used it for more serious shooting instruction.

"The Colt Lightning can be cocked and fired like a single action, or simply squeeze the trigger and the hammer will cycle through and fire the next cartridge. We'll set up some targets now and start practicing. Charlie will help me in coaching each of you. And *remember*," Charity said urgently as she pushed the muzzle of Tina's revolver away from her chest, "keep the barrel where it belongs. If it's not in the holster, point it downrange *at all times*. Do not wave your revolver around like a magic wand. The same applies when we get to rifles. Shotguns are particularly dangerous."

"Are you trying to talk us out of it?" Helen complained.

"No, Helen. Just to keep you from shooting each other," Charity answered tiredly.

Charity's instructions went on for some fifteen minutes. Then she had discarded bottles set out, two for each girl. She gave a final review of aiming and firing procedures and then the order to open up. Charlie broke both of her bottles with one shot each, then assisted in advising the girls on improving their marksmanship. When the last round had been fired—six from each of the six doves— nine bottles remained standing.

"Not too good. Set up some more bottles and we'll try again," Charity ordered.

After three more strings, the quality of their shooting had improved to where only six of the fourteen bottles remained. Charity looked at her shapely pupils and arranged her face into an expression of disgust. Slowly she shook her head and pointed to the surviving bottles.

"Not good, ladies. Not good at all. You have three rounds for each bottle, yet the six of you average one bottle left each. Worse, there's a couple of you that hit neither of yours. We keep working until you get it right."

"It's harder than you'd think," Nichole defended. "We haven't seen you shoot as yet. How do we know you're any better?"

"Yeah, honey. We's standin' out here, broilin' in the sun like buf'lo steaks, an' for all we know, you're no better'n us."

A ghost of a smile flickered on Charity's lips. "I'm glad you brought that up. Though being the two worst shots, I somehow figured you'd get around to it sooner or later."

Without another word, Charity spun rapidly, drawing as she turned, and double-actioned her Lightning. Five of the remaining six bottles became sparkling shards in the air before the echoes died from her six-gun.

Evette's gulping swallow could be heard in the tight silence that followed; then she offered shyly, "You missed one."

Charity drew the hammer to half cock and punched out the five empty casings. "Nope, anyone with good sense only carries five in the cylinder."

"Lord love a duck, honey. I'm sorry I ever asked," the dusky-skinned beauty blurted out.

"As you said, today's rather bad become of the heat. You can see I'm a little off. Left the bottom half of one bottle standing. Now we can get down to the serious work." With that, Charity shucked her left-hand gun and shattered the sixth bottle, then executed a flawless border shift and cleaned off the remains.

They broke at noon to rest under the shade of a large cottonwood. Charity had Tina distribute from a large wicker hamper a lunch of cold fried chicken, with bread-and-butter sandwiches and lemonade. All and sundry ate like starved urchins. After she brushed away the last crumbs, Charity made an announcement.

"This afternoon we'll work with shotguns. Mister Luther Thorne at the bank was kind enough to see we're provided with the correct number. I believe that's his wagon coming now."

"Oh, my," Evette declared with deep feeling. "Shoulder, you're gonna hate me before this day is done."

When the buckboard pulled to a stop, Luther Thorne jumped down before the burly driver set the brake. Lean and spare, with quick movements and bird-bright eyes, he projected his boundless energy as he strode to Charity, hand extended to shake hers.

"Thank you for coming, Mister Thorne," Charity greeted.

"I felt I ought to. Now that those brigands in Cottonwood Springs have stolen the county records again, there's double the reason for someone to go after them. Damned shame it had to devolve on a group of young women."

"Mister Thorne, if your bank puts up a bounty on those records, we'll capture them while we're at it," Charity said confidently while the girls lined up to draw their shotguns.

Chapter Sixteen

Heatwaves shimmered off the ground. Even the birds had been rendered voiceless by the hammer blows of a relentless sun. Not a cloud relieved the brazen-edged blue, and no rain had fallen for a week. After four days of intensive training, the bellicose bawds had developed relatively passable proficiency with rifle, revolver and shotgun. Not heat, nor pain, nor frustrating failure had dampened their resolve.

"We're in this together," Zelda had assured Charity.

Zelda had proven an excellent shot and, along with Charlie, now helped Charity as a coach. Evette had a tendency to close both eyes as she squeezed the trigger. Sudden, sharp commands to open them likewise served to throw her off target, so little could be gained. Charity decided that when the time came, Evette would carry a shotgun. Tina flinched terribly with a revolver, though when she was given a rifle her marksmanship became second best to Charlie's. Over the four days of their training, a small crowd had been attracted to the target range.

Idlers and barflies, cowboys and farmhands enjoying a day off, all trooped out to see the painted ladies break bottles. Quite a number disapproved. After all, they reasonably explained, the girls might wind up applying these new skills to their usual trade. Others saw it as a threat to their masculinity.

"Teachin' women to shoot. Why, next thing you know, they'll be wearin' trousers," an unhappy kibitzer declared one afternoon.

"Worse'n that, they'll be wantin' to vote," an old timer suggested.

The next morning, Charity and her girls appeared in tight-fitting Levi Strauss denims. They had gone on to paper targets by then, on which Charity had drawn the likeness of a man's outline. To many of the onlookers, a disconcerting number of hits occurred in the fatal areas. Particularly plagued by caustic and ribald comments, mostly concerning her size and age, Tina was moved to remark about this.

"Why didn't you make 'em full man-sized, Charity?" Tina inquired loudly. "That way I could shoot off their balls."

The denigrating remarks ceased. Shortly before noon on the fifth day, with drums banging and cymbals ringing, the Decency League of Hopewell descended on the practice ground to lodge a formal protest against this unwholesome activity and the mortifying continued presence of the tainted ladies in the community.

" '*Whaa-aat a friend we have in Je-sus. Take it to the Lord in prayer,*' " dowager throats belted out slightly off key, while the cornet and a newly added German silver flute carried the melody somewhat better.

"Oh joy, just what we need," Zelda complained, coming to her feet after a firing exercise in the sitting position.

"Something tells me there's going to be a change in the schedule," Charity advised them. Rising, she called out to one of the idlers, "Roscoe, go hang up that hindquarter of beef."

"Yes'm. R-r-r-ight away."

Not too bright, but willing, Roscoe hurried to do her

bidding. Charity had taken to bringing extra picnic items for the abandoned half-wit and treated him to licorice whips, horehound drops and bottles of sarsaparilla for helping and cleaning up after their training sessions. In exchange for sweeping out the saloon, the owner of the Idle Hour let Roscoe sleep in the storeroom and gave him cast-off clothing. No one else around seemed to care. As a result he idolized the saloonkeeper and worshipped Charity. A mischievous smile spread on the headhunter's face as she looked back at the "good" ladies of Hopewell.

Among the placards they carried, Charity noted a couple of RIGHT TO VOTE and some DOWN WITH DEMON RUM signs. Apparently not all of the moral framers of Hopewell got the word on what they were to protest. Music blaring, the Decency Leaguers marched to within fifty feet of where the doves stood easily with rifles in the crooks of their arms. When the hymn ended, Amanda Bittles and Mildred Taller stepped out ahead of their following.

"You are a living abomination!" Amanda challenged.

"And you're a deathly bore," Charity gave back. "You're also interrupting our training."

"We've come to see the devil's spawn at play," Amanda informed her.

"You'll not see much 'play' here, Fatso," Zelda jeered.

Amanda went livid. "H-how dare you speak to your betters like that," she raged.

"Who's holdin' the rifle, Tubby?" Zelda demanded archly.

"As to that 'betters' crap," Evette took up, "unless you know twenty-*two* positions for doin' it, you ain't any better'n me, honey."

"Wh-why—why . . . the *nerve!*" Amanda sputtered.

"That's enough, ladies," Charity commanded her charges. For Amanda, she put on her sweetest smile. "You're just in time for a most illuminating phase of our training. I think you'll find it quite practical and highly inspiring. Shall we begin?"

"Put down those devil's tools," Amanda commanded. "Your souls will burn forever if you don't."

"Stack your rifles, ladies," Charity ordered. "Then gather over here. I'll give you detailed demonstrations, then I want all of you to go through the exercises exactly as I show you."

Heartened that she had won her way over the evil firearms, Amanda Bittles motioned to her flock of moral judges to follow her. Boldly she walked to where Charity stood by a hanging quarter of beef, one freshly killed that morning at the meat market. Charity slapped the pliant flesh and then drew her long-bladed sheath knife.

"If you have to take out a guard silently, the best way is from behind. Carry your knife low, gripped so . . . edge in, blade parallel to the ground and level. Approach . . . so. Then whip a hand over his mouth as you plunge the knife into his back, directly through a kidney."

While she described this method, Charity executed the movements, sliding her Greenriver blade deep into the hanging meat. The deadly drabs watched with rapt attention, hands and arms duplicating the moves. Amanda Bittles and several of her stalwart organization turned white around the lips, which slowly changed to a greenish hue.

"What happens if the one you have to silence is sitting down?" Charity inquired rhetorically. "Simple. You come up from behind as before, reach out and give a stout yank backward on his head and slit his throat like this."

Old blood, trapped by the hasty slaughter, oozed out of the wound. Amanda gasped and clutched her stomach. Two of the Leaguers made strange gagging sounds and tottered away to deliver their breakfasts up to the ground.

"Now then, for slashing and stabbing from the front . . ."

At a high gallop, skirts hiked up to clear space for the rush, the ladies of the Decency League departed, cackling and gabbling as they sprinted for the safe and sane world they had left for their ill-advised adventure. Behind them they heard the derisive laughter of the hilarious harlots.

Dallas Avery, appointed by his fellow city fathers as mayor of Cottonwood Springs after the death of Ambrose Slocum, entered the Red Garter Saloon in a state of terrible agitation. He didn't know how exactly to approach the situation he had come to present to Bill Baudine. Consequently it made his receding chin quiver, which gave him the appearance of an imbecile when he stopped at the large green baize table where the gang leader sat taking his midday meal.

"Mu-mister Baudine, there's been considerable complaint among the citizens of Cottonwood Springs lately."

Concho Bill cocked a quizzical eyebrow. "Oh? What is this, Mister Mayor? Ingratitude after we worked so hard to restore the county seat to your fair city?"

"Wu-well, w-we're all grateful, of course. It's only . . . that thu-they have been receiving rather shoddy treatment, don't you think? By some of these, ah, desperados who have invaded our community of late, don't you see?"

Baudine slapped a flat palm on the table, causing his plate and schooner of beer to jump frightfully. "No, I *don't* see, Mister Mayor! Here you come making scurrilous charges against the leading lights of the community and expect me to understand. Spell it out, Mister Mayor. Exactly what is it that offends these carping backbiters?"

"Uh . . . well, ah, there's been some hoo-rawing of our citizens, men and women, uh, sir. Firing at their feet to make them dance, shooting beer mugs out of their hands. Ah, pinching gentlewomen on their, ah, posteriors like common saloon trulls. It's, ah, gone too far."

"No it hasn't. And, between you and me, it's likely to go a whole hell of a lot further. We've lived up to our part of the bargain. Where's the profit we were promised?" Concho Bill challenged.

"You can hardly expect them to pay out of their own pockets," the mayor spluttered.

"If you can't come up with something else, they'd damned well better. These clodhoppers have lived too high for too long. They plow their little furrows and dream of themselves as being free. Well, they're not! They've got to learn to show respect to their betters. *That's* what it's all about, Mister Mayor. R-E-S-P-E-C-T. If they haven't spines enough to stand up for themselves, then these invertebrate slugs had better get used to crawling on their bellies. If you had guts enough to point an accusing finger, Mister Mayor, at whom would you level it?"

"That, ah, D-D-Dandy Spencer. He's the worst of the lot, Mister Baudine," Avery quavered.

"Ummmm. I see." Baudine stroked his smooth chin. "What, exactly, did you come to me for?"

"I had—we, the city council, had—hoped you might intervene. Before there's bloodshed, I mean. The menfolk are getting mighty angry, Mister Baudine. Th-there's even talk of retaliation."

"How?" Concho Bill thundered. "Why do you think we disarmed everyone, you ninny? Unarmed men are in no position to protect their rights. What are they going to do? Do they plan to come after Spencer with pitchforks?"

"There's talk, I've heard some myself, that not all of the guns got turned in. There might be enough for some sort of show of strength."

Dallas Avery would never find out if Bill Baudine paled from anger or fright. The outlaw leader sat a long, silent while, stroking his chin, then pulling the lobe of his left ear. At last he took a deep breath and heaved it out in a prolonged sigh.

"Aaaaah. Well then, perhaps it's time to locate some profitable activity for Dandy and his boys to engage in, something that would take them out of town for a while? Is that what you had in mind?"

Elation and relief flooded through Mayor Avery's body. "Oh, yes, sir. That's a marvelous idea. Could you? I mean, could you really arrange that sort of thing?"

"Consider it done already. They can be on their way tomorrow morning."

Baudine rose, his hand extended for a firm clasp. The mayor took a step forward, reaching out with his own pale fingers. A voice from outside arrested their confirming shake.

"You men. Dandy Spencer, Monroe, the rest of you. Throw down your guns. We want you out of town within an hour. We won't put up with your kind any more."

"What?" the giant bull of a man bellowed. "You're orderin' Dandy Spencer out of town? Look at me. Do I look like a man who tucks his tail and runs?" A mighty peal of laughter followed, ending in the sharp report of a six-gun.

More weapons blazed, men screamed, some whimpered and four townspeople died messily in the dusty street. One of Spencer's gang tottered backward through the batwings, blood gushing from a large exit wound in his back. He fell in the sawdust, halfway to the bar. Old Charlie, the barkeep, peered over the mahogany at him.

"Deader'n a stepped-on toad," he advised the patrons.

"Dandy, over there, that one's still alive. Can I have him?" Monroe asked eagerly.

"Go ahead."

Monroe's Smith and Wesson Russian Model .44 roared, and another townie departed for eternity. Baudine and Avery exchanged glances. The outlaw chief began a slow smile, one that had neither warmth nor humor about it.

"I think there's going to be some more changes around here, Mister Mayor. Some rather drastic ones at that. I'd be hard pressed to try to restrain the boys after that show of bad faith on the part of your townspeople. Fact is, I'd be downright reluctant to try to hold 'em back at all."

"I'm with you, Bill," Karl Richter called from the stable. "I'm with you all the way in this. Way I see it, your friends out there were provoked into a self-defense situation."

"Karl!" Dallas Avery exclaimed, shocked. "You're not siding these—these criminals?"

"In my book, they're not criminals. They can do whatever they want and I'll be obliged to help them out. You'd be smart to change your thinkin', too, Dallas."

"You have all been doing quite well," Charity informed her volunteer posse on the morning of their sixth day of training. "In fact, much better than I expected. Today we'll be shooting from horseback. It's not easy. Actually, unless you come to a stop before aiming and firing, there's little chance, save for luck, for you to hit the target at all. I'm telling you that because I don't want you to lose your confidence when you first try it. Now then," she went on, pacing before the attentive audience.

"We've come to an important stage in learning to fight. We need information on the enemy. That means the time has come to scout out the opposition. Zelda and Charlie will accompany me tomorrow to Cottonwood Springs. Tina will continue shooting instruction for the rest of you while we're gone."

"Won't that be dangerous?" Nichole inquired.

"Our reconnaissance or Tina running the target range?" Charity quipped.

It brought a hearty laugh. Even some of the male spectators joined in. Sheriff Orin Meadows had taken to stopping by for short periods. Each day he appeared a little more downhearted. Today was no exception, and Charity had begun to suspect he'd grown a little more than embarrassed over his hasty decision not to conduct some sort of action against the outlaws in Cottonwood Springs. Let him stew, she thought in satisfaction, though not maliciously.

"We have to have knowledge," Charity went on. "There'll be some risk, but I doubt anyone will recognize me done up in a saloon outfit. I think there are only two who would be positive and we'll have to avoid them. No matter what we encounter, I expect we'll be back here late on Sunday. Now we'd better get to the livery stable and our horses."

At the Red Garter, Dandy Spencer dropped a ham-thick fist on Karl Richter's shoulder. "Startin' to regret you threw in with us?" he growled good-naturedly.

"Oh, uh, no—no, not at all. I—I, ah, just can't quite grasp that, ah, this is my share from the bank job you pulled. Five thousand dollars? For doing nothing?"

"You got Concho Bill and the rest of us into this town. Now they're taken over the stores and everything, he says half share for ol' Karl, so half share you get. Besides, that bank in Meade was easy. Now drink up. Reno's heard you're some kind of poker player. He wants to try a few hands against you." Which, Dandy thought smugly, should soon relieve you of those five big ones.

Bootheels drummed on the boardwalk and the batwings flew open. "Where's Concho Bill?" a hollow-faced individual with a three-day stubble of beard demanded.

"Who wants to know?" Dandy demanded.

"I'm Thane McAllister, one of his riders. Believe it or not, there's a trail herd, all the way from Texas, some ten miles west of here and thirty miles north. Headin' for

Dodge, I reckon. Thought Bill would want to know."

"Damn right he would," Dandy assured him. "Come with me."

Concho Bill Baudine liked the idea right well. He licked his full, sensual lips in anticipation and studied the map on the wall of the marshal's office. He'd taken over the law business in Cottonwood Springs after the pivotal shoot-out with irate townsmen. A quick check on the approximate location of the slow-moving cattle stimulated his thinking.

"Boys, we're gonna go into the cattle business again. We'll take that herd and drive it on to Dodge ourselves."

Chapter Seventeen

A brooding silence pervaded the empty streets of Cottonwood Springs when the hired buggy rolled into town. Few horses stood tethered to tie-rails, and no one with the look of a local resident could be found on the boardwalks. Charity, Zelda and Charlie exchanged puzzled glances.

"No welcoming committee," Charity observed. "Other than those fellows outside of town. It's a good thing we swung around and took the Dodge City road."

"I've a feeling we'll have five rather eager customers later on," Charlie remarked with a mischievous grin. "Those boys acted like they'd never seen a woman before."

"Did you notice the deputy badges?" Zelda asked. "I wonder if they're real?"

"Oh, no doubt," Charity assured her. "Only who might the marshal be? That's what we need to know. Take your pick, girls, it looks like there's four of them," she concluded with a wave around the central business district.

Zelda and Charlie gave a professional examination of the saloons Charity indicated. With a nod, Zelda indicated one. "How about that one? Across from the Red Garter. Osmond's Recreation. I'll bet they could use a star attraction."

"And we're it?" Charity interjected.

"You've got the idea," Zelda told her.

Charity reined in and stopped the buggy. Charlie hopped down and snapped the lead of the land anchor to the driving bit ring on the left-hand horse's bridle. Then, done up in finery and feathers, the trio entered Osmond's Recreation.

Their arrival made the day for Peter Osmond, part owner and bartender. He nearly dropped the heavy beer schooner he was drying when he fixed his eyes on them. His jaw sagged, then instantly snapped closed. A cheery smile, more like a lecherous leer, spread on his moon face. Belatedly he set aside the large pedistal glass and towel.

"Yes, ladies? What may I do for you?"

"Are you the proprietor?" Charity asked, uncertain of how to go about this.

"Part owner. Peter Osmond, at your service."

"May I call you Peter? I'm Giselle, this is Fleur and Babette. We are, ah, looking for employment."

"Unnnh," Peter responded, struck by their combined beauty and the bounty of their bold chests. "Oh, ah, yes—yes. It, ah, could be we, ah, we'd be interested in discussing that possibility. And do, please, call me Peter, Giselle."

Charlie tittered. "What a cute name, Peter-Giselle."

Osmond blushed, flustered in their overwhelming presence. "My—my brother, Don, will be back shortly. Would you care for some refreshment?"

"Thank you. Something cool would be nice," Charity replied. "Do you have any sody waters?"

"Just happen to have some, Giselle. Barley's from back in Emporia. That good enough?"

"It will do fine," Charity told him.

"Flavor?"

Charity's warm, inviting gaze locked with Peter's brown eyes. "Cherry."

When Peter Osmond bent to retrieve the soda-water bottles from a cooler box, he painfully discovered he had a raging erection. He fumbled with the containers a moment, then placed the wire-hinged bottles on the bar and popped them open. Beads of moisture had formed on his upper lip, and his hand trembled slightly as he served them.

"There you are. On the house."

"Why, thank you, Peter," Charity cooed. She was beginning to enjoy this guise she had assumed.

"There must be eight, nine thousand head in that herd," Hal Newhouse observed in an awed tone.

"You've a good eye, Hal," Concho Bill praised his henchman. "At the present going price, that's over sixty thousand dollars on the hoof."

"When do we take 'em?" Hal inquired.

"We want the right time and place. I want to get a look at the ground ahead. Ideally," Baudine enlarged, "we need a bit of a hilly place, with a river ford directly ahead. Less chance of the cattle stampeding that way when we jump the drovers. Within another two, three days, those cows are going to be ours. To do it, though, we're going to need more men. I'm going back with Owen and Frank to Cottonwood Springs for the rest of Dandy's men."

Never had the Osmonds enjoyed such attention from the influx of outlaws, or even the local clientele. News of the three new girls they had hired circulated rapidly. One of those who took particular notice was a new arrival himself, Sunfish Fowler. Fowler had come to Cottonwood Springs in response to Concho Bill's invitation. Not to work with the New Mexico badman, but to take over from him.

At least, that's how Sunfish saw it. He and his men reached the small Kansas town after Baudine's departure to check on the trail herd. The location of Osmond's, directly across from the Red Garter, had been ideal for Fowler's plans. The addition of three lovely ladies only added to his satisfaction.

Within an hour after Charity Rose and her companions went to work for Pete and Don Osmond, Sunfish Fowler and his boys had settled in at the saloon. Fowler sized up the new girls and singled out Charity for his personal attention. He invited her to his table and made short work of the small talk.

"Did Baudine send for you girls?" Sunfish inquired, his outlaw caution seeking the heart of his concerns.

"No. Not exactly," Charity answered. "We, ah, heard about it in Dodge and decided to come have a look around."

"Where's your reg'lar feller to look after you three?" Fowler asked next, still suspicious of their possible connection to Baudine.

"Oh, we don't have us a regular man. We're on our own, so's to speak," Charity spun out their agreed-upon tale.

"Well now, a girl could get into trouble that way. You need someone to protect you, look out for your interests."

Charity leaned closer and laid a hand on Fowler's shoulder. "You looking to fill that spot?" she asked through an inviting smile.

Not expecting such forwardness, Sunfish fumbled his response. "Well, ah, that is to say, er . . . I hadn't exactly thought into that. Now you mention it, though, we could have us some good times, right enough. And, if everything goes right, I'd be in a position to set you three up with a place of your own."

"Really?" Charity came back, feigning excitement. "How'd that be?"

"Best leave that unsaid until the shootin's over." Sunfish gave her a broad wink.

"Whatever do you mean, Sunfish?" Charity prompted.

"This Concho Bill sort of runs this town right now. We got word of a couple of bank jobs lined up, an army payroll on the train. I'm sure you know things change fast in this business. If Baudine can't cut the mustard, there might be someone else in charge, if you get what I mean?"

"Are you wanted anywhere, Sunfish?" Charity asked, keeping it casual, all big-eyed and impressed by this dangerous outlaw.

"Oh, there's a couple of warrants out here in Kansas, one in Colorado. Nothin' so pressing as I can't show my face," Fowler said deprecatingly.

Contriving an expression of ingenuous hero worship, Charity probed further. "Have you got a price on your head?"

"Yep," Sunfish answered, responding to her obvious adulation. "A thousand dollars all together."

"Oh, my, that's a lot of money," Charity stated in an awed whisper.

"More, I hope, than what it costs for your, ah, favors," Sunfish replied as he reached out and lightly brushed one of her breasts.

Charity left his fingers buried in the feathers of her costume as she worked up a regretful expression. "A great deal more, I can assure you. Only . . . well, our timing was bad, it seems. We no sooner got here than I . . . ah, the, er, ah, moon thing." Charity lowered her long, auburn lashes in a show of embarrassment.

"Dang," Sunfish exploded. "How, ah, long?"

"Three more days, maybe. Meanwhile, you can buy me drinks and keep me well fed on steaks and fried potatoes," she added brightly.

"That I'll do," Sunfish promised, eyes alight with lust.

Charity cast a quick glance at Zelda and Charlie. She knew that she would have a hard time keeping them from doing what came naturally, that in fact she had little hope of success. She had to grudgingly admit that such activity provided perfect cover for their visit and to avoid it entirely could create suspicion.

Despite outlaw oppression, Cottonwood Springs boomed on Saturday night. The four saloons grew crowded with thirsty, frolicsome men, both local and visiting hardcases. They drank, gambled and kept the saloon girls busy with endless trips upstairs or to convenient back rooms. Zelda and Charlie were much in demand at Osmond's Recreation. Two fights broke out over whose turn it might be next. Pete Osmond ended both battles with the judicious application of a bung starter.

"I just heard something you ought to know," Charlie informed Charity when she returned from turning a trick with a dusty-haired young gunman.

"What's that?" Charity asked, giving a smiling turndown to an eager customer.

"Remember those cute cowboys we entertained?" Charlie began. "Well, that Concho Bill feller is out of town lookin' at a trail herd, my last john told me. I can't think of any other cattle drive, can you?"

"No, I can't. That means they're in real danger. Baudine wouldn't think anything at all about rustling those cattle. See if you can find out where the herd is, and then we'd better make ready to get out of here."

Within another hour, Charity had all the information she needed. Including that Concho Bill had teamed up with another longrider named Dandy Spencer and that they used the Red Garter as a headquarters. By closing time Charity and her companions were exhausted.

"I haven't spent so much time on my back in a month," Zelda complained.

"It was sure fun," Charlie beamed. "And we're better

off by more'n a hundred dollars." She started counting out gold coins and paper currency into three stacks, one considerably larger than the others.

"That's all yours," Charity told her quickly. "You worked hard enough to earn it."

"Wouldn't look right if we didn't pay you the lion's share, Giselle. Someone might get suspicious, before we had a chance to leave."

"Which we're going to do first thing in the morning. I'll keep it until then, and give it back to you."

Roosters bugled a greeting to the rising sun and the three silent men who rode into Cottonwood Springs. Nothing else stirred on the empty streets, except for a flicker of curtain at a window on the second floor of the Red Garter saloon. By the time Concho Bill Baudine, Owen Percey and Frank Drake tied up outside the barroom, a solitary figure joined them from a side door.

"Trouble, boss," Walney Harper informed Concho Bill.

"Such as?" Baudine asked, his voice reflecting the fatigue he felt intensely.

"Some new girls in town. Said they came from Dodge. But they asked a lot of questions about you. They're workin' over at Osmond's. Real curious they were last night. Also mighty friendly with a feller named Sunfish Fowler, who's sort of taken over across the street."

"Competition?" Concho Bill asked, suddenly alert.

"Might say that. He's got a dozen hardcases with him. Tiny Jim overheard him makin' some remarks about when he ruled the roost. Sorta odd I'd say."

"We'll deal with Mister Fowler when the time comes," Concho Bill said dismissively. "Tell me more about these girls. You say they claimed to come from Dodge? How do you mean that?"

"That's the story they put around. None of the boys

who came here from Dodge know them. Can't recall seein' any of the three in a single saloon there. Then they had 'em a big night, didn't close that place until two this morning. What do you know next but them three are up and around before the crack of dawn."

"Where are they now?" Concho Bill demanded.

"That's what's botherin'. They went to the livery about five minutes ago."

Concho Bill mused on the situation a moment. "I think we'd better pay them a little friendly visit, what say?"

Relieved, Walney Harper grinned. "Sounds like a good idea to me."

Four hard-faced outlaws stalked down the street toward the stable. Small puffs of dust rose from the heels of their boots. In the stillness their approach could be heard like beats on a small drum. Zelda spotted them first.

"Four mean-lookin' jaspers headed this way," she cautioned.

Charity glanced up from harnessing the buggy. "Do you recognize them?"

"No. Three of them at least are strangers. The fourth I sort of remember being around the saloon last night."

Charity came to the front of the barn. A quick look hardened her features. "That's Concho Bill Baudine. Walney Harper's with him. You're right, I saw him in Osmond's last night. Looks like we could be in some trouble."

"Do you know the other two?" Zelda asked as she reached for her six-gun.

"No. If they're with Baudine, they're trouble." Charity gave their situation quick consideration. "We haven't time to finish with the buggy. Get bridles on three horses. We'll go out the back way."

"Saddles?" Zelda asked as she started off to perform the task.

"No time. Hurry."

"Inside the livery," Concho Bill called out. "I'd like you ladies to come out for a moment."

"Answer him," Charity commanded Charlie in a whisper.

"Who's doing the asking?" Charlie hollered back.

"M'name's Baudine. I'm the law around this town. Now come on out where we can see you."

"What for?" Charlie responded to keep the conversation alive.

"There's been some complaints. Men who are missing their pokes. We need to have a little talk about it."

"We didn't do nothin' wrong," Charlie protested.

"Ready," Zelda whispered.

"Come on out or we'll come get you," Baudine demanded, drawing his .45 Colt.

"You've got nothing on us, Marshal. Don't come any closer." Desperation colored Charlie's words.

"This is your last chance," Concho Bill warned.

Charity opened fire.

Chapter Eighteen

Tall plumes of dust erupted from the street near Concho Bill's feet. The bullets whined off eerily. Before he could return fire, he heard a grunt to his left and Owen Percy went down, a slug in his right thigh. Baudine got off a hasty shot and jumped to his left. Another gun opened up from the livery stable.

Dogs set up a tortured howling at the fusilade. Local residents huddled deeper in their beds and hoped the violence would pass them by and soon end. Charlie took aim and clipped the hat off Walney Harper's head with a round from her .38 Colt. Concho Bill's remaining henchmen began to spread out.

"Come on," Zelda insisted. "Now's not the time to collect the bounty on your Baudine fellow. Let's get out of here."

"Right away," Charity agreed as she emptied one revolver and fired two rounds from her other. "Open the back door, Zelda."

Already mounted, Zelda edged her horse forward and swung wide the large double doors. A further obstacle presented itself. They had a corral fence to jump, a scant thirty yards distant. From behind her came two rapid shots and the sound of drumming hoofs. Too late to think about it then, Zelda accepted with resignation.

"Dammit!" Concho Bill exploded into the retreating sound of hoofbeats.

"They're only saloon girls," Frank Drake said, making light of them.

"I'm not so certain," Baudine responded, eyes narrowed. "How many soiled doves you ever known to use anything bigger than a thirty-two pepperbox? Or to shoot so well?"

"Meanin' what?" Drake pressed.

"We could be mixed up with that goddamned female again. Charity Rose. She's been after me for nearly two years. Hell of it is, she's good. Far too good. Now she's got some other women around her who can shoot. Can you visualize the danger that could present?"

"Awh, Bill, you're takin' it all too serious," Frank passed off.

"I don't think so, Frank. Now, we'd better see to getting Owen patched up."

"I still think," Walney Harper put in, "that the big worry is this Sunfish Fowler. No matter how good those women could shoot, they're gone now. Fowler's still in town and on the prod, I'd say."

Harper's words proved prophetic. The quartet of outlaws had walked a block toward the center of town and the doctor's office when three men stepped out onto the boardwalk from the alley beside Osmond's Recreation. Thumbs hooked into the crossed belts at his waist, the one in the middle eased forward two paces and called out to the approaching group.

"One of you Concho Bill Baudine?"

"Who's askin?" Frank Drake demanded.

"Orville Fowler. They call me Sunfish."

"I'm Baudine," Concho Bill declared.

"I hear you're ramroddin' this owlhoot town. Pretty big job for someone your size, ain't it?" Fowler sneered.

"I've handled it so far," Baudine, who was a head taller and a good hand-span wider than Fowler, returned. "Reckon I can keep on top a while longer."

"I've got ten men coverin' the street says you're wrong. Where's your boys?"

Concho Bill began to laugh. "You really think I need help backin' my play against a pip-squeak like you?"

Fowler's face held an amused expression. He raised his left hand and brushed his mustache with the big knuckle of his index finger. "The time'll come when you need them. You can back down now, fight, or I'll give you a chance to think it over."

Concho Bill Baudine drew before Sunfish Fowler's hand came away from his face. His first two rounds went through a window above the saloon door. A man cried out and fell noisily through the remaining glass. By then Walney Harper had his six-gun out and drilled a neat hole through the chest of the man on Fowler's right. Fowler cleared leather a moment before Baudine triggered his third shot.

Hot lead sledgehammered into Sunfish Fowler's chest. Reflexively he staggered back a step, cold numbness spreading behind the initial pain. The Remington .44 in his right hand felt heavy. He let it sag slightly, then jerked it upright to slip-thumb a round. Concho Bill shot him again. Fowler's knees went rubbery, and he slumped back against the front of Osmond's Recreation, a large, wet red smear painted on the whitewash. Although wounded, Owen Percey sat in the dust of the street and pumped shots methodically through second-floor windows. Frank Drake blasted two bullets into the other visible hardcase backing Fowler.

Moaning, the gunhawk went to his knees, tried to raise

his revolver, then toppled backward. In a twinkling, silence filled the street once more. Concho Bill strode forward and hulked over Sunfish.

"Y-you got me straight out an' fair, Baudine," the dying gunman gasped. "I'm a goner for sure. I . . . I hate your guts, but I . . . gotta say you're one damn fine shot."

"You have any last thing you want taken care of?" Concho Bill inquired.

"Y-yeah. Don't . . . don't let the sawbones get hold of me," Fowler requested.

"You can rest easy on that. Anyone you want told?"

"Uh . . . there—there's a gal in Parsons. She's mother to my kid. Send her what my outfit and guns sells for . . . if you . . . please."

"I'll do that," Baudine promised. "I—uh, I dislike sayin' 'I told you so,' but you didn't have a chance."

"I . . . know that now," Fowler admitted. "Damn, oh, damn, it hurts something . . . awfu . . ." Eyes glazing, he gave a mighty shudder and lapsed into eternity.

Wracked with indecision, Charity Rose paced the floor of her room in the hotel at Hopewell. The herd and the men driving it were in danger. She wanted to do what she could to save them. She also wanted to get a crack at Baudine and free the people of Cottonwood Springs. With the lure of the trail herd drawing Baudine out of the town, the latter could be accomplished easily. If the sheriff would only cooperate.

Sheriff Meadows could take a large posse and occupy Cottonwood Springs in the gang's absence. Then it would be an easy matter, she reasoned, to drive them off when they returned from their rustling. That would leave her and her small army of female gunhawks to hit the outlaws in the flanks and rear. What she had to do, she reluctantly admitted, was to face the possibility of another rebuff and take her case to the sheriff. Appeal to him again for help.

Sheriff Orin Meadows looked up from his morning edition of the Topeka *Capitol Journal* as Charity, Charlie and Nichole entered his office. "What can I do for you, ah, ladies?" he asked with only a slight tone of condescension.

Quickly, yet patiently and in detail, Charity laid out what had been discovered on the clandestine visit to Cottonwood Springs. Slowly she built her case, at last revealing the danger to the trail herd. Orin Meadows listened with undivided attention. Occasionally he nodded or pursed his lips. At last the tale ended. The lawman took a deep breath.

"Well now, Miss, ah, Charity. I allow as to how a saloon girl might hear any number of things from the men she encounters in her, ah, line of work. Some of it might even deal with criminal acts, past or future. Which lends considerable credence to what you've said. Since you can verify that there is such a trail herd, my course of action is clear."

Excited and relieved, Charity brightened. "Then you *are* going to ambush them at Cottonwood Springs?"

"No. I'll form a posse and ride to the general location of the Texas drovers. We'll do our best to prevent the rustling, and drive off the outlaws in the process."

"What about capturing Bill Baudine?" Charity asked, all of a sudden worried over the quality of the offered action.

"If we can," Meadows answered lightly.

"What about the county records?"

"That's another matter, entirely not your concern," the lawman answered primly. "It should be left up to the court to decide."

"I'm going with you. We, ah, all are."

"You certainly are not, young lady," Meadows snapped.

"But we can help. I've worked hard to train these girls in how to shoot, to hit what they shoot at and to ride horseback."

"No man in his right mind is going on a posse with a . . . with a . . . a band of Hookers Girls!" the indignant sheriff blurted.

"So that's it, eh? I'm damned sick and tired of this, Sheriff. And I don't feel constrained to put up with it any more. Wire the sheriff of Havupai County, Arizona Territory, Mark McDade. He'll verify this," she went on as she removed from her purse the deputy's badge she carried.

"I'm a duly sworn deputy of Havupai County, a bounty hunter, and I have no intention of losing my interest in Bill Baudine because of some stupid pseudo-dislike of prostitutes. I'm not one, goddammit, and these girls aren't any longer. I demand the respect my position deserves, or . . . I'm tempted to call you out over it, Sheriff."

Red-faced, his fist slamming the desk, Sheriff Meadows half rose. "If you weren't a woman, by damn, I'd be tempted to accept that challenge."

"Now we've gotten down to it," Charity seethed. "It's all a matter of our sex. Not what we do with it, but that we aren't of the proper one. It's a man's world, they say. Well, I don't happen to believe that. We're going to do what we feel is necessary in this situation and if you don't like it, you can shove it up your . . ."

"Get out!" Meadows thundered, drowning out her last word.

At the hotel, Charity didn't present such a positive attitude. Quite to the contrary, she had a hard time convincing the girls from taking off at once for the cattle drive. Even pessimistic Helen came out in favor of the prospect.

"They're dear, sweet boys and someone's got to help," she declared. "Outlaws trying to steal their cattle, some of them might get hurt."

"Yes, we should be riding there right now," Nichole urged.

"We can't, don't you see?" Charity responded. "Sheriff Meadows isn't taking this lightly. He'll have us all in jail if we do anything before he and his posse leave town. I'm a peace officer. I can't deliberately break the law by throwing down on the county sheriff. We have to bide our time, be more clever than Meadows or Concho Bill. Planning is what will pay off."

"Don't you want to get back at Baudine?" Nichole queried. "After him shooting at you and all, I'd think . . ."

"*We* did most of the shooting, dear," Charity reminded her.

"Yes, but . . . it's still not right just sitting around here doing nothing."

"The sheriff will be gone in an hour. Once they're gone, we can make preparations to go to Cottonwood Springs. Someone has to free the people there and deny the town to Baudine's men. When that's done, the rest should be easy," Charity told them. "The sheriff wouldn't listen to me on that point. Now that he's going after the rustlers, it's up to us to take their headquarters away from them. With the posse at their heels, they'll be in a cross fire."

"That's Crooked Creek up ahead, Bill," Tiny Jim Boyle informed his boss. "Those cows are backed up for more than a mile."

"Perfect. We'll hit 'em now." Baudine rose in his stirrups to outline his strategy. "Some of you spread out to the west some. We'll go in in a fan shape. Start picking off the drag riders from as long a range as you can. We don't want the cattle run too much. I want six, eight of you to hold back and try to keep the stupid critters milling, don't let 'em line out into a run. The rest move on the cowboys. We don't need to kill 'em all, but make sure they're knocked out of the saddle. Run off the remuda. Then we can start moving the cattle. Get going!"

Within ten minutes the first of the drag riders came into view. Carefully placed shots blew them off the backs of their horses. The detonations caused the nearest cattle to set up a frightful lowing. Two cowboys spotted the killers and returned fire.

Bullets cracked past Concho Bill's head. He swung to one side, reined in tightly and snapped off a round that caught one of the defenders in the shoulder. He went sprawling over the rump of his fidgeting mount. Several cows bolted, spraddle-legged, then ran full tilt into the milling herd.

Their actions excited others to panic. Bellows of surprise and pain came from the huge gather. From a distance, shouts gave the alarm. Baudine's men swept along the flanks of the herd, rifles and six-guns blazing at the unprepared cowboys.

"Rustlers!" Peter Norton shouted as he ducked low in the saddle and drew his revolver.

"We're being attacked," another drover took up the cry.

"They're everywhere!" a third lamented a moment before a two-hundred-fifty-grain slug cleaned him from the saddle.

A quarter of the herd had reached the far bank, or swam the shallow creek at a gravel ford. Excited by the gunshots, those behind rammed into the wading animals, creating further confusion and panic. The surprised drovers lost control and turned helplessly to find themselves confronted by smoking firearms. Several threw up their hands in surrender.

For their efforts they got clubbed with rifle butts. Grover Dalton, flanked by Peter Norton and four other hands, offered stiff resistance. For a while they held off the determined outlaws. Dalton put a bullet through the head of one bandit, levered a round into his Winchester and tracked another. Peter shot a horse out from under a reckless hardcase. The animal shrieked in pain as it crashed into the hard ground.

A moment later, its late rider cried out in sheer agony as the frightened cattle surged away from the center of gunfire and sharp hoofs tore and pounded at his chest. From a low rise, a fusillade of outlaw fire whipped into the defenders. Grover Dalton grunted, clutched his stomach and fell from his horse. Peter rushed to his side to protect the man he most admired.

In the same moment, the last thread of control snapped and the cattle ran wildly through the stream and off, pursued by shrilly yelling rustlers. They left behind a terrible shambles.

Chapter Nineteen

Some sort of brightness — could it be sunlight? — made orange circles on the inside of his eyelids. His head throbbed powerfully, and his ribs gave off a fiery ache along the right side. Was there pain in Heaven? Before making an effort to open his crusted eyes, Peter Norton felt about him and encountered wiry tufts of grass. No, not dead after all, his senses reported. Vastly relieved, Peter tried to sit up.

Numbing waves of pain washed through his body, awakening a surge of nausea that called forth a hollow groan. The unseen world whirled around him, and a moment of panic further disoriented Peter when he tried, and failed, to open his eyes. With the thumb and index finger of his left hand he felt of the crust that glued the lids tightly. The sharp grains loosened gradually, and Peter opened first one, then the other stinging orb.

"My God!" he gasped aloud in a fearful croak.

Vision blurred, the ground around Peter appeared to be broken up into small mounds. Slowly he began to focus and recognize the humps to be dead horses, cattle and men. After a long, uncomfortable wait, Peter attempted to stand, only to fall back. From a short distance he heard a soft groan. Someone else was alive. He made another effort, which also lacked success, then settled for crawling on hands and knees. It seemed to take an eternity to reach the side of the cowboy who had given sign of life.

"Doake . . . Doake, are you . . . can you hear me?" Peter grated out.

Eyelids fluttered, and Doake Stevens recoiled violently from Peter's touch. Then his eyes opened and he licked dry lips. "Uh . . . Petey. We've got to . . . where's Mister Dalton?"

"I don't know," Peter answered. Slowly he looked around. "He was over on that side of the herd." *The herd!* Recollection startled Peter. "What happened to the cattle?"

"Run off. We was hit by rustlers, Petey. Don't you remember?"

"Oh . . . no. Not everything. Can you move?"

"I'll, ah, try," Doake responded. Face pinched in pain, he slowly sat upright, then came to his knees. Then he made a great effort and stood over Peter.

"Give me a hand," Peter asked.

With both of them on their feet, they made slow progress over the pounded ground toward the far side, where more bodies formed grisly mounds. Among them, they located Grover Dalton. To Peter's great relief, they discovered he still breathed. Slowly the trail boss's eyes opened, glazed blue marbles gazing uncomprehending at Peter and Doake.

"Mister Dalton, it's Peter. Can you hear me?" Peter urged, lifting the man's head.

A soft moan answered him, and Dalton slowly blinked his eyes. Then a weak hiss became words. "I hurt . . . awful. M'belly burns."

Peter examined the rancher's gut wound. A purple-green bulge of intestine protruded from the bullet hole. Peter's stomach lurched at the sight, yet he desperately wanted to do something. Tears wet his eyes. Though he'd never admit it, never put it in words, he loved Grover

Dalton as the father he'd never really known. Dalton coughed and the bit of intestine pulsed obscenely. Don't die, Peter pleaded silently.

"What can I do, Mister Dalton?" Peter begged urgently.

"Gut-shot, right enough," Grover Dalton diagnosed. "Get a canteen. Wet a bandanna and lay it over the hole. That's what we did back in the War. Hurry, boy."

Despite his own injuries — the flesh scrape along his ribs had started to ooze blood again — Peter complied with alacrity. The makeshift dressing in place, he moved the canteen to Dalton's mouth, but the trail boss weakly pushed it away.

"Never give a gut-shot man a drink, that's what Hood's surgeon always said. Some make it that way, some don't."

"Y-you're gonna make it, Mister Dalton," Peter replied in a strangled tone, one more of pleading than assurance.

"That slug tore up something inside mighty bad, Petey. I . . ."

"We got two more alive over here," Doake shouted.

"Good," Peter answered. "That makes five of us."

"An' no horses," Doake responded sadly.

Eight miles northeast, nearing the sandhills of Meade County, the rustled cattle had calmed and been tightly gathered. Hal Newhouse rode up to where Concho Bill Baudine sat his horse atop a small knoll and reported.

"We've got a crew fairly well lined out, Bill. We found the old bellwether and she's got the herd strung along the trail in good order."

"Fine. If the weather holds and Frenchy does a good job on forging those bills of sale, we should have an easy time of it. Have we got a rough talley?"

"Eight thousand, eight hundred and some, the way I hear it."

"Our lucky day," Baudine replied dryly.

"I was wondering," Newhouse went on. "After we sell these cows, are we going back to that town?"

Concho Bill mused on it less than five seconds. "Cottonwood Springs is growing a bit too hot for my liking. Let the others who have moved in have it."

"And the consequences later on, eh?" Newhouse added with a smirk.

"That's it exactly, Hal. With the amount of money we'll have on hand we can do some tall celebrating in Kansas City, then head back to our old stomping grounds. I sort of miss that old pueblo in Cañon de los Aparajitos."

Newhouse snickered. "Oh, sure. And the *mujeres* you brought up from Mexico don't have a bit to do with it, I bet."

"Certainly not," Bill replied jestingly. "A woman's a woman. Like rocks and flies, they can be found anywhere."

Frenchy Descoines had sat silently beside Bill Baudine. Now he leaned toward his old friend, a worry wrinkle creasing his high, smooth forehead. "What about that Rose woman?"

"To hell with her. She can keep on chasing shadows in western Kansas while we enjoy ourselves three hundred miles away," Bill declared in a lighthearted manner.

Doake Stevens managed to get a fire lighted. He put water on to boil and cleaned the wounds of the others, saving his own for last. Peter helped him. Together they cared for Grover Dalton. The older man had grown more pallid over the half hour since Peter revived him. His breathing was shallow and irregular, and his skin burned in one place while being icy in another.

"Peter," Dalton summoned, unaware that Peter sat cross-legged, holding the dying man's head in his lap.

"I'm right here, Da—uh, Mister Dalton," Peter answered instantly.

"Peter, son, I'm a goner sure's there are cow pies in a pasture. I want . . . I want you to know . . ." A fit of coughing broke up his words.

Peter held him tightly and bathed his forehead with a damp cloth. "Easy, easy now. You're going to be all right."

When the wracking spasm subsided, Dalton raised a feeble hand and gestured vaguely in the direction of the others. "I want someone to come listen to this."

"That's not necessary, Mister Dalton," Peter suggested.

"Yes, it is. Now call 'em over," the stubborn old man insisted.

"Doake, can you, Len and Carter come over here?" Peter called out.

It took a few minutes, and when the survivors had gathered, it appeared that Grover Dalton had sunken further. Peter sat in shocked silence as the words came forced from his employer's laboring chest.

"I want you all to listen close and bear witness when needed. All three of my sons are well provided for. They have spreads of their own and are prospering. I . . . I've always thought of Petey as my son, also. When you recover the cattle—and . . . and I know you will—I want wages paid to the families of the dead, and to all of you. The rest of the money, and my holdings on the Brazos, I want to go to Petey Norton. Th-this is my dying declaration. See that it is carried out as I wish." Coughing wracked him again, and he turned his head sideways to vomit out a stream of blood and bile.

"No, Mister Dalton, no," Peter cried wretchedly. "You don't need to do that. Besides, you're gonna live though this. I—I won't let you die!"

"God's . . . got a bigger say in it than . . . you do, son," Grover Dalton forced out, the ominous sound of a death rattle deep in his throat.

"Oh, no, please, please hold on," Peter begged, a small, frightened child again.

A series of brief, violent spasms shook the man in his arms. Grover Dalton tried feebly to reach up and touch Peter's tear-streaked face, then let his arm drop back. "G'd-bye . . . s-s-s-so—"

For over half an hour Peter wouldn't let anyone remove Grover Dalton's body from his lap. He sat rocking and staring with still-blurred vision across the undulating Kansas prairie. The sun had lowered far in the west when the battered survivors buried their former boss. Their grief-burdened hearts chilled at the thunder of rapidly approaching hoofbeats as Peter Norton patted the last shovel of dirt into place. Two of the drovers had their sidearms out before they realized the oncoming band of men had no hostile intent.

"Sheriff Orin Meadows, Crowley County," the leader identified himself. "I know I'm outta my jurisdiction, but I heard you might expect trouble and we rode to try to prevent it. Sorry we didn't get here in time. D'you lose many?"

"Twenty-three men," Peter announced bitterly. "In-including the trail boss and owner of the herd. Cattle all rustled."

"That's too bad, too bad," the sheriff commiserated.

"The bastards cut down fellows when there was no need at all. Butchered us. Everyone's wounded. You gonna go after them, Sheriff?" Peter appealed.

Meadows covered his mouth with a gloved hand for a long moment, then shook his head. "Afraid not, son. We're stickin' our necks out now, way it is. We can take you back to Hopewell, over Crowley County way. Only a thirty-five mile ride."

"Who takes care of this?" Peter's anguish spilled over. "Who goes after those sons of bitches?"

"We'll bury the dead for you," Meadows offered. "Do it

right now, then head out in the morning. As to chasin' the rustlers, they're probably over the line into Ford County by now. If not they soon will be. Still another jurisdiction . . ."

"Fuck jurisdictions!" Peter shouted in his hurt and bafflement. "We want those bastards hung and the cattle returned."

"Now, now, take it easy, son. We'll work on it. That's all I can promise you at this time."

Due to the injured men, they traveled slowly. Sheriff Orin Meadows brought the survivors from the cattle drive back to Hopewell at seven-fifteen the next evening, an hour short of sunset. With him he brought news of the rustling, which set the town a-buzz. Stunned at the terrible slaughter done, though relieved that Peter had missed such an awful fate, Charity took the news to her bevy of bawds.

"All of them dead?" Nicole asked in an injured wail. "All but those four?"

"I'm sorry, Nichole. Yes, they are the only survivors. Peter, Doake, Len and Carter," Charity sadly confirmed.

"Someone's got to take care of them," Charlie suggested, tears in her eyes.

"We will!" four of the soiled doves declared at once.

"Yes. Let's do it," Tina enthused. "They'll need a place to stay and to get well. We can do that."

"What about Cottonwood Springs?" Charity asked archly.

"With the outlaws gone with the herd, we can do that any time. This way we have more time for planning," Zelda suggested.

"Now, that's the first sensible thing I've heard out of any of you since we came back from there," Charity told them. "I'll tell Doctor Levins that we can make room for them here. That'll mean you girls will have to double up, of course."

"Well, ah, we hadn't exactly looked at it that way," Tina informed her. "We sort of figured on, ah, doubling up with those poor cowboys."

"And what? Love them to death? They're wounded, shot full of holes. There's such a thing as too much tender care."

Her menagerie looked shocked, as though such a concept had never occurred to them before. Then Zelda began to laugh. Her whoops and hearty bellows proved contagious, and as she wrapped one arm around Charity's shoulder, the others joined in.

"I've got to hand it to you, honey, you sure draw some interesting pictures. We'll go easy on them, mind. Hot soup and back rubs and maybe just once in a while a little, ah . . . yeah."

An hour after Doctor Barnes finished treating the wounded cowboys and saw them established in comfortable beds in the hotel, Charity slipped into Peter's room. Her ears still rang with the protests of the hotel owner, Leonard Ransom.

"I ain't turnin' this hotel into a hospital. Dangit, Doc, I know you've always wanted a clinic of sorts for this town, but this ain't the place," the hotelier bellowed as the injured walked through the lobby and started up the stairway to the soiled doves' rooms.

"What do you expect them to do, Leonard? They can't get healed sleepin' on the damned bandstand," Dr. Levins snapped at him.

Their crusty banter had provided the first light moment for Charity since she learned of the disaster. The smile remained fresh on her lips as she crossed the room and sat on the edge of Peter's bed.

"Hello, Petey," she said throatily, her husky voice emphasized by emotion. "Are you resting all right?"

"I, ah, I was before, ah, well, you always manage to get me . . . get me . . . awh, you know," he ended miserably, his healthy young male reaction to her heady aura of femininity embarrassing in light of his grief.

Charity bent and kissed him soundly on the lips. "I wouldn't care so much for you if you didn't," she told him lightly. Her hand slid under the cover and encircled his suddenly rigid penis. "When you're feeling better, we'll have to do something abut this," she promised. "For now, sleep and get well."

"What are you going to be doing?" Peter asked, aroused, yet fighting it.

"What I came here to do. I'm going to work out some way to get Concho Bill Baudine and the rest for what they did."

"You?" Peter couldn't believe her statement.

"Oh, Peter, you never knew. I . . . well, I'm not a working girl, that you know. I'm . . . I'm a bounty hunter. I swore to get revenge for my father's murder by the Baudine gang and I mean to finish it now, here in Kansas."

"My . . . God," Peter blurted with a note of astonishment.

Chapter Twenty

Dust hung over the bedding ground as the outlaws-turned-drovers prodded the dim-witted animals into motion. A bloated orange ball hung on the eastern horizon, its warming rays stirring swarms of savagely biting face flies that served to remind many why they had chosen the owlhoot trail instead of an honest means of making a living. Concho Bill Baudine stood beside the chuck wagon, which the gang had managed to save intact. He carefully read over the papers prepared by Frenchy Descoines.

"I'd swear these are genuine, Frenchy," Baudine praised. "Right down to the embossed seals. You've now made me the proud owner of eight thousand, eight hundred ninety-seven prime Texas cattle.

"Thank you, *mon ami*. With less than fifty miles to cover to Dodge City I can already smell the precious scent of gold."

"Riders comin' in," one of the headers called out.

Concho Bill squinted as he looked up the trail, then smashed a blood-filled fly that had become too involved in feeding on his lip. Frenchy's keen eyesight soon picked out detail.

"Red legs."

"What?" Baudine inquired of his second in command.

"I suspect they are of those known as, ah, Jayhawkers. They've come to shake us down or seize our cattle," Frenchy informed him.

"Isn't this fine irony? Here we nearly break our necks in a night raid to rustle these critters; now along comes someone who wants to cheat us out of the herd."

"Hallo, the camp!" one of the approaching riders sang out.

"Hello!" Concho Bill called out. "Come on in, but we'll meet and talk over on that knoll. Don't want to spook my cows."

"All right," came the reply.

"Frenchy, you get some of the boys ready. Too bad now that we sent Dandy Spencer and his bunch back to Cottonwood Springs."

"*Oui.* They could prove most handy in a situation like this," Descoines replied, eyes alight with planning for a special reception.

On the low knoll, Concho Bill met the self-proclaimed State Livestock Inspectors. He maintained a sardonic smile while they rattled off their pat little spiel.

"We're here to check your road brand, original brands and the health of your animals. Can't have any of that tick fever getting loose in Kansas, ya know."

"How do you know these cattle are from Texas?" Bill asked like a real owner.

"They got the look, mister. If we find any infected animals, the whole herd will be quarantined."

"I, ah, find that unacceptable," Baudine told them, sudden iron in his tone.

"There ain't much you can do about it," the moon-faced, red-necked man in bib overalls stated flatly. "It's the law. Without our certificate you can't sell your herd anyway."

"Let's get down to it without a lot of haggling. How much is that health certificate going to cost me?"

"Oh, not so much as to take all your profit. Goin' rate's four bits a head."

"Half a dollar? Have you been chewing peyote buttons? There's no way in hell I'll pay that much."

"Then your herd's confiscated as of now," the chubby extortionist announced. His fat right hand patted the butt of a Remington revolver slung at his hip. The belt and holster appeared humorous compared to his great bulk.

Concho Bill's eyes narrowed. "How do you propose to enforce that?"

"We've got more men over that rise. One shot and they'll come in here a-hellin'. After that, you'll be on your way to the county jail."

"Oh, they'll get their one shot, all right," Concho Bill assured him, consulting his big turnip Ingersol watch. "Only I don't think it'll turn out the way they or you expect."

"Mister, you're in Kansas and we're the law here," the obese blackmailer ground out. "You'll do what we say."

"I doubt that," Concho Bill stated flatly. "That you're the law and that we'll do as you say."

To underscore his resistance, a flurry of gunshots came from beyond the rise. A horse screamed in frantic pain, and men's voices rose for a moment. A few more shots sounded, dull thumps that didn't disturb the herd, and then silence returned.

"If I'm not mistaken, that was the termination of your posse's venue. I'll put it in simple words for you. You ain't got anybody to back you."

Frenchy Descoines rode his dappled Andalusian to the top of the ridge and signaled with his hat. All taken care of. Concho Bill produced a big smile.

"Now it's going to give me the great pleasure of killing you," he informed the confused Jawhawkers.

Baudine had already filled his hand, the muzzle of his .45 Colt swinging level with the Jawhawker's stomach. The outlaw leader slip-thumbed the first round, which smacked into the wide expanse of lard before him. The redleg grunted and completed his draw.

Concho Bill shot him again. This time the bullet entered the man's left lung only an inch above his heart. Quickly Baudine changed targets and blew one shakedown artist off his saddle with a dead-center slug to the chest. The third rider threw up his arms in surrender.

"You're thieves and extortionist bastards," Concho Bill growled. Then he shot the man between the eyes.

Peter Noonan showed considerable improvement by afternoon of the next day. His vision had cleared, although the headache remained. Dr. Levins suspected Peter might have had his skull cracked by the rifle butt that had slammed into his head above his left ear. The bullet scrape along his ribs had scabbed over, and the physician decided no sutures would be needed. The young cowboy appeared quite cheered when Charity visited him at two o'clock.

"You're looking fresh enough to get out and around," she observed in a light tone.

"If you had my headache, you wouldn't be saying that," Peter responded. "Though that's all that hurts now." A sudden warmth radiated from his loins. "I, ah, I sort of hoped you came to, ah, take care of that something we talked about yesterday," Peter croaked out, his vocal cords in the grip of the powerful emotion he felt.

Charity smiled sweetly and removed her riding jacket. "I, ah, sort of hoped you hadn't forgotten about it," her husky voice proclaimed.

A prominent elevation in the bedding proclaimed his willingness. Peter felt as though a thousand feathers tickled him. Every sense had been heightened and even the dull throb of his head receded in the presence of urgent passion. He threw back the blanket and sheet to reveal his bare, bandaged chest and the thick bulge in his long-john bottoms. Charity had the buttons of her blouse undone.

"We'll have to take it easy," she prompted. "Don't want to open those cuts again."

"Oh, bother those cuts," Peter answered with effort. Charity's soft, warm touch on his chest brought forth a groan. "Char—Char, I'm on fire."

"Ummmm. Hold the blaze back awhile, Petey," Charity instructed. "I have to get out of these boots."

At last the campaign could be launched, Charity thought expectantly as she clattered down the stairs the next morning. Sheriff Meadows' posse was long gone, her plans checked and rechecked. She had left Peter's bed shortly after dawn, dressed quietly and went to alert the fallen angels. They received the news eagerly. Particularly Charlie.

"We'll take that town and finish ol' Baudine before anyone knows what's happening," she predicted cheerfully.

Now, abristle with weapons, the seven bawds and their

leader carefully packed saddlebags with dynamite sticks, fuses and blasting caps. Several early risers stood around, some gaping in consternation. Knives, six-guns, rifles and shotguns had been stowed away when Charity announced that they would take time for breakfast.

By twos, the small, heavily armed force walked their mounts to the tie-rails outside the corner café. Inside they ordered ample, filling meals and ate every scrap. That accomplished, Charity paid for them and they filed out. A larger crowd had gathered.

"Think any of them would try to stop us?" Helen asked, always suspicious.

"That's like asking if the little boy wanted to wrestle the bear," Charity answered.

At seven o'clock, by her father's big turnip watch, Charity swung a leg over Lucifer's back and eased into the saddle. "Let's ride, ladies," she commanded simply.

To the heartening cheers of some Cottonwood Springs refugees, the party trotted out of town.

Peter Norton awakened in a cat-lazy return to consciousness. He felt the sheet beside him to discover Charity had departed at some earlier hour. He felt drained, and a buzzing warmth filled his body. A prodigious stretch brought a wince of pain as it put pressure on his flesh wound. He'd not do that again, he reminded himself. His bladder gave insistent warning, and Peter swung his legs out of bed. When he got to a sitting position, his eyes fixed on the small oblong of folded paper. "Dearest Petey," it read.

I have chosen to inform you by this note, rather than in person. The reason should be simple. You are in no condition to accompany us, so I wanted time enough to put distance between us. I hope by the time you read this we will already be in Cottonwood Springs. When the fighting is over, I shall return to you.

> All my love,
> Charity

"Damn!" Peter exploded aloud.

Despite his tenderness and a slow, intermittent throb in his head, Peter dressed, strapped on his cartridge belt and left the room. By the time he reached the street, his strength had stabilized and he walked like a man unharmed. Near the corner he accosted five men discussing the early morning departure of the female posse.

"You should be ashamed," Peter challenged. "Standing here gossiping like old women while those young girls are out there fighting your fight. What sort of men are you?"

"Well, er, ah . . ." one stammered, refusing to meet Peter's eyes.

"What can we do, mister?" another equivocated.

"You could form a posse and ride after them. They're headed for Cottonwood Springs and God knows how many outlaws are still there, armed and ready."

"You're one of those fellers got shot up by rustlers, right?' a tall, lean man inquired.

"That's right. And I'll tell you one thing. If there's not something done about it, I'll go after them alone."

"Now, you don't need to . . ."

"Right. I shouldn't have to, but I will. Who'll join me? C'mon. Go gather up some men willing to fight and let's run that bunch out."

"What about the county-seat records?" the lean one asked.

"We can get them while we're there. Don't just stand there, go round up some others."

Half an hour later, Peter Norton led a posse of twenty men out of Hopewell. Although a bit light-headed, he showed no other effects of his injuries. Within him burned a solid determination to reach Charity's side and protect her in the upcoming battle.

Chapter Twenty-one

Eight women dressed in mannish-style riding outfits trotted along the main street of Cottonwood Springs. In their wake silence settled, broken only by the distant call of a meadowlark. Farther along, stray mongrels yapped their challenges, only to grow quiet and slink away, tails between their legs. Better-cared-for dogs next set up a racket, only to be hushed by their unseen masters. A tiny, bright coin in the clear Kansas sky, the sun struck flashes of brilliance off the many weapons they carried. When they neared the business section, several idling outlaws took interested notice.

They began to whistle and call out ribald suggestions to the grim-faced women. Several made bawdy jokes, and laughter carried down the street. The auburn-haired leader of the silent women signaled a halt. Several hardcases noticed a large, fierce-looking dog at her black gelding's feet. One of the hard-bitten men took a step off the boardwalk and touched a hand to his hat brim.

"Y'all come to help us rob a bank?" he asked sneeringly.

"No," Charity Rose answered levelly. "We came to serve you notice that your time has run out. Gather your gear and be out of town within an hour."

This pronouncement elicited enormous peals of hilarity. Road agents and bank robbers slapped their thighs and stomped their boots. The self-appointed spokesman confronted the women once the snickers subsided.

"How do you propose to enforce that?" he smirked.

"If you're not out of here by then, we'll shoot you down like the dogs you are," Charity informed him. "Get going and spread the word like we are."

A sudden realization struck the outlaw as he studied Charity's face. "Sa-a-ay, you're the one Baudine said to look out for. Chestnut hair, green eyes, a damn big dog. Sister, you done come to the wrong place."

His Merwin and Hulbert .44 Pocket Army cleared leather ahead of Charity's Lightning. Before he raised it to her level, the lighter .38 barked twice. Dark spots appeared on his chest, yet the six-gun continued its upward arc. Charity shot again, hot lead entering his left eye socket.

Jellied by hydrostatic shock, his brain turned off. Even so, his trained reflexes triggered the big revolver in his right hand. The bullet cut through the air slantwise in front of Charity's chest and sent her rust-colored Stetson flying, a neat hole in the brim. Charlie and Zelda opened up a fraction of a second later.

"Slow, ladies," Charity told them as the rode on past the sprawled corpses of four men.

"What do you mean, 'slow'? I'd didn't expect him to draw," Zelda protested.

"You should have. That's why you were slow," Charity calmly answered as she inserted fresh cartridges into her six-gun.

Six men ran from the Red Garter. The sight of eight women, dressed as men and calmly reloading, set them off stride. Charity raised her hand with her reloaded Lightning and called to them.

"You men are on warning. You have an hour to leave town or die like those fellows down the street."

"Like hell," one defiant hardcase rapped out as he drew.

Charity shot him in the hollow of his throat. At once four six-guns, two rifles and a shotgun blazed around her. The six outlaws lay kicking feebly in the dust. A lone gunman charged out the batwings of the Red Garter, only to do a frantic, midair reversal and propel himself back inside. A load of buckshot from Evett'e Parker took out most of the louvers in the swinging doors. A deep, soulful groan followed, and the same man staggered out streaming blood from face, chest and abdomen to fall face-first on the boardwalk.

"Let's clean that rat's nest out," Charity commanded.

She, Zelda, Charlie and Evette dismounted and started toward the front of the saloon. Curtains moved in a second-floor window, and Charity called a warning a fraction of a second too late. A Winchester barked and brought a thin wail of pain from Zelda as the bullet gouged along the top of her left shoulder. She went to her knees, clutching at the profusely bleeding wound.

"Get under the overhang," Charity commanded. She turned to Zelda, helped her upright and shoved her roughly forward. "It's all right, it's only a crease in your flesh."

"It stings like ants chewin' on me," Zelda gulped out.

"Most likely. Here . . ." Charity removed a checkered bandana from around her neck and wound it over Zelda's shoulder. "Cover the place from the doors. We're going in."

"How?" Zelda asked.

Charity answered with a grin and picked up a weathered captain's chair, which she hurled through a huge, painted-edge window. On the opposite side of the batwings, Evette did the same with an empty beer barrel. Weapons blazed, and then they crisscrossed each other and darted in through the doorway. Caught unawares by this tactic, the outlaws inside fired at the windows and died for their mistake. Charlie entered last and shot a man halfway up the curved staircase.

In the sudden silence, his sommersaulting body made loud thumps as it rolled down the steps. Charlie Finn, the bartender, waved a white apron from behind the bar, his large, heavy body and handlebar mustache well out of sight.

"Hey, I only work here. Don't shoot," he called out.

"Who's in here, besides the ones we splattered all over your bar?" Charity demanded, not yet giving Charlie leave to stand up.

"T-two, three fellers upstairs."

"Where's Concho Bill Baudine?" Charity demanded.

"Not here. He an' his boys are with a herd of cattle they rustled," Finn answered hastily.

"Damn," Charity muttered aloud. "I hoped we'd catch him here. Stand up," she said louder. "Let's see your hands empty of everything but that apron."

"Sh-sure, lady," old Charlie muttered unsteadily.

A rattle of gunfire sounded from outside, and a man cried out sobbingly for his mother. More shots, then a long pause.

"We got four more, Charity," Tina shouted gleefully.

"Good shooting," Charity answered back. "Keep your eyes open. There'll be more."

"Char—Charity Rose? You're the one Baudine talked about?" Charlie Finn asked in awe.

"I suppose I am," she told him. "Who is in charge when Baudine's gone?"

"Dandy Spencer. He's over at the hotel," Finn informed her.

"Thank you so much. Evette, Charlie, let's go take those men upstairs, then we'll head for the hotel. Zelda, if anyone moves down here, blow them in half," Charity ordered over her shoulder.

Nearing the top of the stairs, Charity ducked low when a hail of hot lead shattered plaster and chipped the wood of the banister. She motioned to Charlie, who worked her way quickly back down the stairway. Charity and Evette retreated to the landing and waited.

"Don't shoot, Zelda, it's me, Charlie," the young whore announced as she started for the door.

A minute later she returned with a fused stick of dynamite in one hand. Charlie Finn took a look at it and groaned, hands over his eyes.

"Oooh, nooo," he pleaded.

When Charity accepted the deadly cylinder, she slit the end of the fuse with a fingernail and fished a lucifer match from her shirt pocket. She snapped it to life and touched the flame to the raw end of braided cord. Sparks erupted and the odor of burning powder filled the stairwell. Her six-gun holstered, Charity hurried to the top tread in a low crawl and hurled the sizzling device down the hall.

Two shots blasted the stillness, then a deep male voice bellowed, "Oooh, God! It's dynami—"

The blast numbed their bodies, blanked their ears, and left the salty-sweet taste of exploded dynamite on the lips of the three young women on the stairs. Charity shook her head in an attempt to rid it of ringing, then gestured for the pair to follow her.

In the upper hall, a dazed man stumbled through the plaster dust and smoke, a six-gun held limply in his hand. He looked up at the clatter of boots against fallen lath and tried to fire a shot. Charlie pumped two rounds into his heart before he had a chance. In the room he had exited they found another man, unconscious, bleeding from nose and ears. Parts of a third man grimly decorated the shattered ceiling and walls at the far end of the hall, where bright light came in through a huge hole.

"Looks like we're done here," Charity announced calmly, as she tried to fight down a rising tide of nausea.

Out on the street, Charity directed her vengeful Valkyries toward the hotel. "Three of you go around back. There's bound to be more than one door."

They found the lobby empty. "Butch," Charity commanded, putting the half-wolf on search, *"sireadh."*

Nose close to the floor, Butch methodically sought fresh human spoor. Many weaker scents teased his sensitive sense of smell, which he ignored. Near the stairway, his hackles rose and he tossed his head from side to side.

"Thuas, Butch, *thuas,"* Charity ordered, and up Butch went. When he neared the top, she called out again, *"Fan!"*

Butch froze. Charity motioned to Evette and Charlie, and the trio ascended the staircase. Charity's keen hearing picked up the thump of bootheels and the soft click of a lock mechanism. A faint squeak betrayed the opening of a door.

"Marbh, Butch," Charity commanded. *"Marbh!"*

Freed of restraint by the command to kill, Butch launched himself with powerful haunches and shot down the darkened hallway. A moment later there came a grunt, followed by a terrible scream. The shrieks of agony continued while Charity and Charlie mounted the last treads and hurried toward the sound of the violent confrontation. Butch, his muzzle red and wet, met them in the open doorway. Charlie took one look at what lay beyond him and turned away, gagging.

A man lay there, one leg drawn up, fang-shredded fingers still clutching futilely at his ravaged throat. Charity felt weak in the knees at the gruesome scene, and her own stomach lurched as she heard the sound of vomiting behind her. Simultaneously, Charlie and an unseen gunhawk fired, and the young prostitute dropped to the floor.

Less than a second later, Charlie discharged her six-gun again. "He missed me, but I got him," she said proudly. She rose and wiped at her chin. "Let's find some water;

my mouth tastes awful."

Making slow progress, the trio went the length of the hallway, kicking in each door in turn. In two cubicles they found frightened, legitimate customers, trapped there since the outlaws had taken over the town. These they directed down the stairs toward relative safety. At the far end, overlooking the street, they came upon Dandy Spencer and Reno.

"We've got no quarrel with you ladies," Dandy said through a scowl. His curly brown hair and boyish features gave him a winning quality.

"That's right, miss," Reno added. "We're willing to cooperate to the fullest."

"Were you in on the cattle rustling?" Charity demanded.

"No," Dandy said without hesitation. "I was here in town, and so was Reno. Some of my boys went along. Why?"

"You may have saved your lives," Charity told him curtly. "Can you tell me who it was gut shot the trail boss and injured a young boy, white-blond hair, slender build?"

"Ummm. I can't say for certain, miss," Dandy responded after a moment's consideration. "But I think it might have been Clell Brockman. He runs a small outfit, joined up for the raid on that trail herd."

"How can I know you're telling the truth?" Charity demanded.

Dandy produced a lopsided smile. "You can't. But I am. I happen to believe that livin' is a whole lot better than bein' dead."

Charity lowered the hammer on her double-action Lightning and rubbed the warm barrel along one cheek. "You've got that much . . . for the time being, at least. Now shuck those weapons and come along peacefully to the marshal's office."

"Now, that wasn't part of the bargain," Dandy protested. Three six-guns turned black muzzle holes to his face. "On the other hand, we can always arrange to get out on bail. Lead the way, ladies."

"No, *you* lead, we'll follow," Charity ordered. "*Claon*, Butch."

Butch took his position at her heel, alert and watchful as the men disarmed and walked dejectedly from the room.

With Dandy Spencer and Reno locked in jail and the rest of his gang either accounted for or off with the herd, there remained little to do, Charity considered. The first thing would be to find Clell Brockman. Not a face showed on the streets when Charity and her deadly drabs started out from the marshal's office. From two blocks away, sunlight glinted off a rifle barrel that protruded from the belfry of the church. Acting on well-honed instinct, Charity spread her small army out, and they advanced along three parallel blocks.

Fifty yards from the church, the hidden marksman opened up on Charity and Tina. His first rounds cracked through the air a safe distance from either woman, and Charity answered with three fast rounds.

Two of them struck the big bronze bell. It tolled discordantly. The next shot from the sniper struck a building front, far off target.

"That's it," Charity seized instantly. "Aim for the bell, Tina."

Tina's Winchester cracked with authority. Two—three—four rounds whammed into two smaller bells. From the other two streets, shots sounded also, and the bells replied in numbing notes. Charity sighted on the big one and fired one Lightning dry. She holstered that gun and quickly sent two more slugs from the other into the vibrating bronze tocsin.

Instantly a terrible howl of human agony came from the bell tower. A rifle clattered over the lip of the open belfry window and fell to the shattered ruin on the ground below. Only a moment passed before a human figure came into sight, hands clasped to his ears.

He wavered there a second, and then Tina fired again. Struck in the chest, the hardcase staggered backward and fell against the bell. His wail of pain turned into a shriek of terror as he slid down the smooth surface and dropped headfirst through the cutout in the floor. The scream cut off with a sickening, wet-sounding smash.

The door to the vestry flew open, and a man's figure launched itself from the top step. Charity fired at him while he was still in the air. A weak cry came from the gunhawk, and he collapsed when his near-side foot touched the ground. A spreading red stain on his thigh indicated where Charity had placed her bullet. Quickly she and her companions closed in on him. Colt Lightning at the ready, Charity knelt at his side.

"What's your name?"

"C-Clell Brockman," he answered her.

"We've been looking for you, Mister Brockman. If you'd like to live awhile, you can answer my question. If not, I'll drop you right now," Charity told him menacingly.

"You wouldn't kill an unarmed man, would you?" Brockman wailed, only to find his words cut off by the muzzle of a Colt Lightning shoved into his mouth.

"You nearly killed a boy I think very dearly of, and you did kill the man he worshiped like a father, you son of a bitch. If there's no reward posted on you, there's no reason for me to keep you around, dead or alive. So answer my questions and I might let you go. Is Bill Baudine with the rustled cattle?"

Fear glowed in Brockman's eyes. When Charity pulled

the gun muzzle from his mouth it made a little popping noise. Brockman swallowed with difficulty.

"Yes. He and his whole gang. He sent us back and I've got the idea he's not coming back here."

"Where's Karl Richter?" Charity demanded.

"I don't know who you mean."

"Richter, the man from town who's behind it all," she bored in.

"I—I still don't know him," Brockman protested.

"I'm right behind you," Karl Richter said as he ratcheted back the hammer of a Colt .45.

Charity froze a moment, then turned slowly.

"That's it. Move slowly, lay down that six-gun. All of you, do as I say."

Once Richter had them disarmed, he relaxed a little. So much so that a loud whoop and the thunder of hoofs from down the street distracted him with a nervous start. It gave Charity the opportunity to dive for her abandoned Lightning. At the same time, she called to Butch.

"Grabh é!"

Butch took him on the right side, sharp fangs digging into Richter's forearm. The greed-driven merchant howled and went to his knees. His Colt revolver fell from numbed fingers. Charity came up with her Lightning and commanded Butch out so she could have a clear field of fire.

"Butch, *amach!*"

"Get him off me," Richter wailed even after the big dog released his savaged arm.

"Mr. Richter, you're under arrest, in case you didn't know it. Give me half an excuse and I'll kill you," Charity informed the bitten man.

"Charity!" a clear, high voice called out.

Charity recognized Peter's white hair and slight build. His posse streamed into town, discovering the battle to have ended. They gathered around the victorious bawds and clamored at them with questions.

"What do we do now?" one of the rescuers asked.

"The records," came a quick answer. "Let's get the county records."

A cheer went up and in a whirl the men of Hopewell dashed off toward the courthouse. Peter Norton remained behind.

"What now, Charity?"

"Bill Baudine is with the herd. From the way it appears, Sheriff Meadows isn't doing a hell of a lot about it. We're going after them."

"And I'm coming along," Peter said forcefully.

Charity started to protest, to cite his recent wounds, then bloomed into a ready smile. "You'll need a fresh horse," she told the youth.

Chapter Twenty-two

Fine particles of grit hung in the air around the nine people who rode northeast through the sandhills of Meade County. The incessant southwest Kansas breeze caused the irritating bits to hover around them, invading eyes, nostrils, ears and mouths, itching in body creases. Their horses snorted in protest.

"We can't be too far," Charity Rose stated confidently after she signaled for a halt.

"She's right," Peter Norton added. "Cattle only move ten, twelves miles a day. We passed the place where they jumped us an hour and a half ago."

"We'll give the horses a fifteen-minute rest, walk them out," Charity commanded. "Then push on."

Mounted again, the small posse topped a low, rolling ridge, dotted with gray-green blobs of sage and Spanish bayonet. To Charity's surprise and consternation, they came suddenly upon Sheriff Orin Meadows' posse. Although it was still a good three hours before sunset, the men were going about the chores of setting up camp.

"What are you doing here?" Charity demanded of the lawman when she and her companions rode up.

"I could ask you the same thing, missy," the Sheriff snapped back.

"We left Cottonwood Springs at eight-thirty this morning," Charity informed him. "That was *after* we jailed or ran off the outlaws."

"Sheriff, that herd can't be more than five miles away," Peter Norton put in. "Why are you stopping here?"

"Well now, I . . ." Meadows dissimulated. "After all, we are out of my jurisdiction, you know."

"If I didn't know better, I'd think you didn't want to catch them," Charity accused.

"Now see here, I've been pushing these men hard. They . . ."

"How hard, Sheriff?" Peter Norton challenged. "We got here from Cottonwood Springs in less than a day. You've been on the trail of the rustlers for nearly three."

"What do you expect me to do?" the embarrassed lawman asked.

"I'll tell you what you're going to do," Charity interjected. "Also how you can make sure it works." Quickly Charity outlined her plan.

"Shooo! Shoooup!"

Flank riders called and whistled to the cattle, keeping them in a line of four abreast with flicks of quirts or a slap on the rump with a coiled rope. The outlaw drovers wore bandanas over their mouths and noses, eyes tightly squinted against the powder-fine miasma of sand that was churned up by the thousands of hoofs. Out ahead, Concho Bill Baudine and Frenchy Descoines halted their mounts and leaned back in their saddles. With a hand on their horses' rumps, one arm supported each of them as they looked back at the herd.

"Another day and we'll be in sight of Dodge City," Frenchy predicted.

"Better make it two days," Bill amended.

"I'll welcome a bed to sleep in," Frenchy announced. Then he stiffened, came more upright and pointed over the bobbing heads and horns of the cattle. "Someone coming fast, Bill."

"Could be the law, do you think?" Bill queried.

"If it is, they took their time getting here," Frenchy observed. "Want me to take some of the boys ahead and set up a little ambush?"

"It would sure help, but I don't think we have time," Baudine said dryly.

Puffs of white smoke could be seen from the nearer riders, and over the steady rumble of pounding hoofs, the sound of shots came to Frenchy's ears. One of the drag riders pitched forward in his saddle.

"Damn!" Baudine swore. "If they stampede these cattle, we could be in some trouble."

"Do something Bill, those *cochons* are serious," Frenchy stated urgently.

Concho Bill had counted nine riders. Not a large force for his men to take on, yet with the cattle to control, it cut down on how many he had to put up a defense. He quickly evaluated the situation. It wouldn't do, he decided, to let this hostile force get in among them. He'd have to take the fight to them. Half a dozen riders lazed their way along ahead of the herd, oblivious to the danger because of the incessant bawling and clash of horns. He signaled to them, then pointed toward the charging attackers.

"Those cattle are going to break at any moment," Frenchy warned.

"Get the men to the other side. We'll try to keep the

herd between them and those people."

Frenchy rode at once to carry out Baudine's commands. The six riders, accompanied by their leader, turned to confront the attackers. A flurry of shots crackled through the air. Cattle bellowed and balked. Then, with the swiftness of a tornado, they bolted in a dozen directions.

"There go the cattle!" Peter shouted.

"I see it," Charity answered. "Keep your mind on those men riding toward us."

To emphasize her words, Charity reined in and fired two quick shots from her Marlin Pacific. The second of her big slugs smacked into the chest of one outlaw, who wavered in the saddle for several strides, then toppled to one side. Panicked cows turned him into pulp.

"They've lost control," Charity shouted to her posse of lovelies. "Now, if only . . ."

A thunderous fusillade erupted on the far side of the herd. From the top of a rolling dune, Sheriff Meadows' posse opened up with murderous accuracy. Hal Newhouse and Dan Meeker fell from their saddles, followed by Willie Hansen. The sudden appearance of reinforcements arrested Concho Bill's charge. He turned about and waved frantically for his surviving gang members to break off and run for it. Charity fired again, and a searing path burned along Baudine's right shoulder near the base of his neck.

Semiconscious, he fell forward, frantically gripping his horse's neck. Frenchy Descoines grabbed Bill's reins, and the two outlaws galloped away.

"Get after them!" Charity shouted.

"The cattle," Peter interjected.

"We'll get them later," Charity commanded. "I want Baudine dead."

Strung out over a mile, the outlaws raced in hopes of escape. Charity and her soiled doves sped after them. Quickly mounted, the sheriff's posse divided into two groups, one to try to contain the cattle, the other to join the pursuit. Billows of dust obscured the chase, and individual bandits died horribly, mouths choked with dust. Charity drummed past a riderless horse and fingered empty loops in search of another cartridge for her rifle.

She had to shift her weight in the saddle to put the rifle in the scabbard, losing precious ground to the outlaws. Evette, looking unhappy that the range had prevented her using her shotgun, loped up beside the auburn-haired avenger.

"They gon' run those horses into the ground," the darkhaired prostitute predicted.

"We can hope so," Charity answered back.

Twenty minutes passed in the uneven contest; then, on the horizon, Charity saw the crumbled outline of an old barn and what might have been a house. Before she could call it to her companions' attention, the surviving outlaws veered in that direction and urged more speed from their flagging mounts. Charity yanked the hat from her head and waved it in that direction.

"They're going to hole up over there!" she shouted over the thunder of hoofbeats.

Already Zelda, Charlie and Nichole had swerved their mounts to follow. At a hundred yards, the outlaws opened fire. At fifty yards, their shots became more accurate. Helen uttered a shrill cry and slumped onto her horse's neck. Tina managed to rein in and capture the uncontrolled animal. Helen roused slightly and dismounted with difficulty. Blood smeared the front of her shirt and the saddle skirt. The impetus had gone out of their charge, and the rest dismounted. To her relief, Charity saw Helen assume the sitting position and take up a rifle.

Return fire slowed the outlaw defense. Sheriff Meadows arrived with half of his men and spread out to surround the dilapidated homestead. Gunshots crackled for some twenty minutes. By then both sides considered it a stand-off. The end would come when one faction or the other ran out of ammunition. Charity decided to alter the odds somewhat.

"Come with me," she summoned Charlie and Tina as she fished another box of rifle cartridges from the left-side pouch. "Bring the dynamite from your saddlebags, Charlie."

From her own, Charity took fuse and detonators. Then, keeping low and advancing in rushes, the trio circled to where the barn blocked them from the house. Using her belt knife, Charity quickly cut slits in six sticks of dynamite and crimped detonators to cut fuse with her teeth, then inserted the fused caps. She wrapped waxy string around the incisions and set the hastily constructed bombs on a corral rail.

"Like at the saloon," Tina declared through a grin.

"Only this time we want to do a little more damage," Charity replied. "Charlie, you take three sticks and I'll get the others. We'll go through the barn and throw them from the front. I'll go up in the haymow."

"What'll I do?" Tina asked, feeling left out.

"You put down covering fire from one of the windows," Charity told her. "All right, ready?"

A sagging door creaked as Charity pulled it open. She

was surprised that none of the gang had taken positions inside. Then she saw a boot-clad leg. Several apparently had, only to be eliminated by Sheriff Meadows' posse. With added caution Charity started for the flat strips of board, nailed to an upright, that formed a ladder to the loft. The musty odor of rotted hay wrinkled her nostrils. Dust drifted down through cracks in the loft floor. Charity and the two girls froze and listened for any sound of footsteps.

None came, and Charity signaled them to move on. She reached the improvised ladder and started up. A board creaked in protest. Instantly a shot blasted from above. Charlie and Tina fired upward, splintering the planks overhead. Another ringing crack signaled their inaccuracy. Charity clung to the rung above her and hoped the man wouldn't rush to the opening.

Dust and straw trickled down between the boards as the unseen gunhawk took two steps. Charlie and Tina blazed away again. Charity heard a soft grunt, and then the barn shook to the thump of a fallen body. Charity looked down at her companions.

"That's the way to do it. Thanks."

Four more rungs and Charity made it to the loft. A low pile of rotting hay lay in one corner, with a considerable deposit strewn over the flooring. Without hesitation, Charity approached the front. Metal screeched as she pulled the latch in the small hatch set in the big loading door. Wincing at the thought of the taste, she took a short, thin cheroot from her jacket pocket and set it alight with a lucifer. She puffed on it a moment to build a decent coal, then studied the tip. With one hand she reached for a stick of dynamite. The other she used to push open the hatch.

No shots sounded immediately, and she breathed

deeply with relief. Charity poised herself, lit the fuse and hurled it through the window. It spun end over end through the air, trailing sparks, then landed on the edge of the roof. She saw another one arc over from below, where Charlie stood. That stick fell short by five feet.

Ba-Ba-WHOOM! The explosives detonated nearly simultaneously. Bits of the sod-and-shingle roof flew into the air; dust and smoke filled the barnyard. Charity grabbed up another piece of dynamite and touched the cigar to the fuse end.

"Throw harder, Charlie," Charity advised before heaving her deadly missile.

Rapid crackles came from the facing side of the house. Bullets cracked through the wood close to Charity's head, and she flinched away reflexively before remembering the sputtering fuse in her hand and throwing with flawed accuracy. The stick landed under a window.

A moment later it went off with a frightful roar. Glass blew inward, and the sash fell from its casing. Muffled voices cursed inside the house. Charity lighted and threw her last stick.

It struck the bare window casing and hesitated a brief moment before it tipped inside. Charlie's final dynamite bomb sailed through the opening. Men shouted in fear and boots thumped on sagging floors. A moment later both sticks went off. The wall bulged, then came apart in a shower of bits, from the size of a dust grain to a six-foot chunk that slammed down noisily halfway across the barnyard. Men began to scatter in a panic.

They raced for a shallow draw where their horses had been tethered. Shots followed them from three quarters of the circle. Charity emptied one .38 Lightning and headed for the stairs. Before she reached the floor, Tina and Charlie rushed out the front doors.

"Wait!" Charity cried.

A rifle cracked as she reached the opening, and blood and brains splashed out the back of Tina's head. The running girl stopped short, turned part way around and fell on her face.

"Tina! Oh, Tina," Charity cried out in anguish.

Another rifle blast sounded, and Charity felt a powerful impact in her shoulder. Numbness followed; then she looked up. She immediately spotted the hardcase who had wounded her and shot the fifteen-year-old prostitute, and calmly emptied three rounds from her left-handed Lightning into his chest. His knees went slack and he fell, the smirk of his kill-lust wiped from his face. Other posse members had joined the rush on the house.

From inside, voices called out that all the outlaws left were dead. Only those who escaped to the gully remained. In the whirl and confusion, Charity looked around and could not find Peter. A dull ache throbbed in Charity's right shoulder as she hurried from one group to another.

"Have you seen Peter Norton!" she asked of each.

At last Hiram Weeks, a deputy badge twinkling on his vest, came to her. "He was the first in the house, Miss Charity. I—I never saw him after that."

"You at the house!" a voice called from the ravine. Charity recognized it as that of Bill Baudine. "We've got a tow-headed kid over here, looks to be about fourteen, fifteen. Let us go peacefully or I'll scatter his brains all over this gully."

"Turn him loose, mister. He's just a boy," Sheriff Meadows ordered.

"He'll bleed like anyone else, Sheriff."

"Bill Baudine," Charity called out in cold, deadly anger. "This is Charity Rose. If you harm that boy, I'll cut off your balls and feed them to you."

"You bitch!" Baudine shouted back, rage supplanting reason. "You taken to sleeping with babies now?" Another taunt died on his lips as Charity placed a shot within six inches of where his voice came from. After a protracted second, he spoke again. "Let us ride out of here or I'll kill this kid right in front of you."

"How many are you?" the sheriff inquired.

"You're not dealing with him, are you?" Charity demanded, incredulous.

"Of course I am. That boy's life is at stake."

"No, dammit. This is my chance to finish off Bill Baudine and his slime," Charity complained.

"There's four of us," Baudine answered. "Everyone else is dead or too bad hurt to ride. Agree to it, Sheriff, or so help me, the yonker dies."

Tears streaking her face, Penelope came to where Charity stood. Charity held a bandana compress in her left hand, pressed tightly to the wound in her shoulder. "Ch-Charity, Evette is dead, and Helen bad hurt."

"Tina's gone, too," Charity told her, heart heavy and cold.

Leaden words, hot and aching, formed in her mind. Evette, Tina; would Peter die, too? Did he have to? Bitter in her personal defeat, Charity nodded to Sheriff Meadows. "Let them go, Sheriff."

"Ah, what changed your mind?" the lackluster lawman inquired.

"There's been too much killing. Too many good folks have died. I can hunt down Baudine later on. I can't let him harm Peter."

"It's all right, Baudine. You and your men ride out," Meadows called out.

Fuming impotently, while Penelope bandaged her shoulder, Charity watched while Concho Bill Baudine,

Frenchy Descoines, Tiny Jim Boyle and Rupert Hayes rode out of the ravine and started off toward the west. Bound tightly hand and foot, Peter Norton had been slung over his own saddle, while Hayes led the animal along.

The entire posse looked on grimly as the outlaws walked their mounts out of the gully. Unspeaking, they watched in contempt while the enemy mounted up and cantered off as though on a Sunday stroll. In three minutes, they reached a point well beyond range. There, Concho Bill rode back to the pack animal and yanked Peter roughly from its back. After he dropped Peter to the ground, Bill gave a cheerful wave and cantered away.

Charity's anger had been driven beyond bounds. She immediately swung atop the nearest horse and galloped out to the hog-tied youth.

"Petey, did they hurt you?" she shouted anxiously before she dismounted.

He could only nod his head. Quickly she cut Peter free, then went to capture his horse. When they returned to the posse, Charity had a grim look. "We're going back to the herd. Peter and I and his friends from the drive are going to take over from the sheriff's men and see the cattle are taken care of properly."

"What about us, Charity?" Charlie asked, tears running freely for her fallen sisters in sin.

"You did well, girls," Charity told them. "I'm proud of you. And I feel so awful that Evette and Tina were killed. I'm going on now. I'll collect on the rewards from Dodge City. You girls go back to town, and I'll send you all an equal share in the bounty money. That way you can get along until you find something decent to do."

"We can't," Nichole wailed. "We don't know what to do without you, Charity."

"Nonsense. Now listen to me. If you can take a town away from outlaws and recover a stolen herd of cattle from rustlers, there's nothing you can't do. All you need is to set your minds to it. You're brave, intelligent and determined. That's all anyone needs in this life. So find something, stick to it and you'll all do well. Good-bye now."

To tearful farewells, Charity and Peter rode off after the missing cattle. Miles melted away, but the images of her army of soiled doves remained strong. There would be two, perhaps three days to Dodge City and a lot of loving with Peter, she considered. Yet it would be a long time before she forgot Zelda, Charlie, Helen, Penelope, Clarisse, Evette, Nichole, Adrianne and Tina. They would, she felt sure, warm her heart for years to come.

And some day, somewhere, she would settle with Concho Bill Baudine.

Author's Note

The county-seat wars raged in western Kansas from 1867 to 1889. Land speculators, called Boomers, purchased huge tracts of land, organized a development company and initiated town sites. Then they advertised in the East and as far off as Ireland, Germany, Poland and the Russian Ukraine. As immigrants poured in, the town lots sold for increasing prices, as did the dry farmland. Power, wealth and longevity went to the town that became the county seat. Rival communities hotly contested this honor and created for the Kansas Supreme Court nearly a hundred years of litigation. The last case was settled in 1953. Events portrayed in this volume regarding William Barclay (Bat) Masterson and James Marshall in the siege of the Cimarron courthouse are real. For purposes of story we have telescoped the event into an earlier year and different season. The actual event took place in January of 1889. For those interested in pursuing it further, good accounts can be found in several Kansas histories, as well as in biographies of Bat Masterson and Billy Tilghman, and in *The Shooters* by Leon Metz, Mangan Books, El Paso, Texas, 1976.

—EJH

SADDLE UP FOR ADVENTURE WITH G. CLIFTON WISLER'S TEXAS BRAZOS!
A SAGA AS BIG AND BOLD AS TEXAS ITSELF, FROM THE NUMBER-ONE PUBLISHER OF WESTERN EXCITEMENT

#1: TEXAS BRAZOS (1969, $3.95)
In the Spring of 1870, Charlie Justiss and his family follow their dreams into an untamed and glorious new land—battling the worst of man and nature to forge the raw beginnings of what is destined to become the largest cattle operation in West Texas.

#2: FORTUNE BEND (2069, $3.95)
The epic adventure continues! Progress comes to the raw West Texas outpost of Palo Pinto, threatening the Justiss family's blossoming cattle empire. But Charlie Justiss is willing to fight to the death to defend his dreams in the wide open terrain of America's frontier!

#3: PALO PINTO (2164, $3.95)
The small Texas town of Palo Pinto has grown by leaps and bounds since the Justiss family first settled there a decade earlier. For beautiful women like Emiline Justiss, the advent of civilization promises fancy new houses and proper courting. But for strong men like Bret Pruett, it means new laws to be upheld—with a shotgun if necessary!

#4: CADDO CREEK
During the worst drought in memory, a bitter range war erupts between the farmers and cattlemen of Palo Pinto for the Brazos River's dwindling water supply. Peace must come again to the territory, or everything the settlers had fought and died for would be lost forever!

Available wherever paperbacks are sold, or order direct from the Publisher. Send cover price plus 50¢ per copy for mailing and handling to Zebra Books, Dept. 2261, 475 Park Avenue South, New York, N.Y. 10016. Residents of New York, New Jersey and Pennsylvania must include sales tax. DO NOT SEND CASH.

BEST OF THE WEST
from Zebra Books

THOMPSON'S MOUNTAIN (2042, $3.95)
by G. Clifton Wisler

Jeff Thompson was a boy of fifteen when his pa refused to sell out his mountain to the Union Pacific and got gunned down in return, along with the boy's mother. Jeff fled to Colorado, but he knew he'd even the score with the railroad man who had his parents killed . . . and either death or glory was at the end of the vengeance trail he'd blaze!

BROTHER WOLF (1728, $2.95)
by Dan Parkinson

Only two men could help Lattimer run down the sheriff's killers—a stranger named Stillwell and an Apache who was as deadly with a Colt as he was with a knife. One of them would see justice done—from the muzzle of a six-gun.

BLOOD ARROW (1549, $2.50)
by Dan Parkinson

Randall Kerry returned to his camp to find his companion slaughtered and scalped. With a war cry as wild as the savages,' the young scout raced forward with his pistol held high to meet them in battle.

THUNDERLAND (1991, $3.50)
by Dan Parkinson

Men were suddenly dying all around Jonathan, and he needed to know why—before he became the next bloody victim of the ancient sword that would shape the future of the Texas frontier.

APACHE GOLD (1899, $2.95)
by Mark K. Roberts & Patrick E. Andrews

Chief Halcon burned with a fierce hatred for the pony soldiers that rode from Fort Dawson, and vowed to take the scalp of every round-eye in the territory. Sergeant O'Callan must ride to glory or death for peace on the new frontier.

Available wherever paperbacks are sold, or order direct from the Publisher. Send cover price plus 50¢ per copy for mailing and handling to Zebra Books, Dept. 2261, 475 Park Avenue South, New York, N.Y. 10016. Residents of New York, New Jersey and Pennsylvania must include sales tax. DO NOT SEND CASH.

THE UNTAMED WEST
brought to you by Zebra Books

ILLINOIS PRESCOTT (2142, $2.50)
by G. Clifton Wisler
Darby Prescott was just fourteen when he and his family left Illinois and joined the wagon train west. Ahead lay endless miles of the continent's rawest terrain . . . and as Cheyenne war whoops split the air, Darby knew the farmboy from Illinois had been left behind, and whatever lay ahead would be written in hot lead and blood.

TOMBSTONE LODE (1915, $2.95)
by Doyle Trent
When the Josey mine caved in on Buckshot Dobbs, he left behind a rich vein of Colorado gold—but no will. James Alexander, hired to investigate Buckshot's self-proclaimed blood relations learns too soon that he has one more chance to solve the mystery and save his skin or become another victim of TOMBSTONE LODE.

LONG HENRY (2155, $2.50)
by Robert Kammen
Long Henry Banner was marshal of Waco and a confirmed bachelor—until the day Cassandra stepped off the stagecoach. A week later they were man and wife. And then Henry got bushwhacked by a stranger and when he was back on his feet, his new wife was gone. It would take him seven years to track her down . . . to learn her secret that was sealed with gunpowder and blood!

GALLOWS RIDERS (1934, $2.50)
by Mark K. Roberts
When Stark and his killer-dogs reached Colby, all it took was a little muscle and some well-placed slugs to run roughshod over the small town—until the avenging stranger stepped out of the shadows for one last bloody showdown.

DEVIL WIRE (1937, $2.50)
by Cameron Judd
They came by night, striking terror into the hearts of the settlers. The message was clear: Get rid of the devil wire or the land would turn red with fencestringer blood. It was the beginning of a brutal range war.

Available wherever paperbacks are sold, or order direct from the Publisher. Send cover price plus 50¢ per copy for mailing and handling to Zebra Books, Dept. 2261', 475 Park Avenue South, New York, N.Y. 10016. Residents of New York, New Jersey and Pennsylvania must include sales tax. DO NOT SEND CASH.

SWEET MEDICINE'S PROPHECY
by Karen A. Bale

#1: SUNDANCER'S PASSION (1778, $3.95)
Stalking Horse was the strongest and most desirable of the tribe, and Sun Dancer surrounded him with her spell-binding radiance. But the innocence of their love gave way to passion—and passion, to betrayal. Would their relationship ever survive the ultimate sin?

#2: LITTLE FLOWER'S DESIRE (1779, $3.95)
Taken captive by savage Crows, Little Flower fell in love with the enemy, handsome brave Young Eagle. Though their hearts spoke what they could not say, they could only dream of what could never be. . . .

#4: SAVAGE FURY (1768, $3.95)
Aeneva's rage knew no bounds when her handsome mate Trent commanded her to tend their tepee as he rode into danger. But under cover of night, she stole away to be with Trent and share whatever perils fate dealt them.

#5: SUN DANCER'S LEGACY (1878, $3.95)
Aeneva's and Trenton's adopted daughter Anna becomes the light of their lives. As she grows into womanhood, she falls in love with blond Steven Randall. Together they discover the secrets of their passion, the bitterness of betrayal—and fight to fulfill the prophecy that is Anna's birthright.

Available wherever paperbacks are sold, or order direct from the Publisher. Send cover price plus 50¢ per copy for mailing and handling to Zebra Books, Dept. 2261, 475 Park Avenue South, New York, N.Y. 10016. Residents of New York, New Jersey and Pennsylvania must include sales tax. DO NOT SEND CASH.